Edison's Gold

GEOFF WATSON

EGMONT
USA
NEW YORK

EGMONT

We bring stories to life

First published by Egmont USA, 2010
This paperback edition published by Egmont USA, 2013
443 Park Avenue South, Suite 806
New York, NY 10016

Copyright © Geoff Watson, 2010
All rights reserved

1 3 5 7 9 8 6 4 2

www.egmontusa.com

THE LIBRARY OF CONGRESS HAS CATALOGED THE HARDCOVER EDITION AS FOLLOWS:
Library of Congress Cataloging-in-Publication Data

Watson, Geoff.
Edison's gold / Geoff Watson.
p. cm.
Summary: Tom Edison and his friends become embroiled in a mystery involving
his "double-great" grandfather's inventions, a secret society, and a vendetta being
carried out by a descendant of inventor Nikola Tesla.
ISBN 978-1-60684-094-8
[1. Adventure and adventurers—Fiction. 2. Secret societies—Fiction. 3. Inventors—Fiction.
4. Edison, Thomas A. (Thomas Alva), 1847–1931—Fiction. 5. Tesla, Nikola, 1856–1943—
Fiction. 6. Mystery and detective stories.] I. Title.
PZ7.W3268Ed 2010
[Fic]—dc22
2010011312

E-book ISBN 978-1-60684-471-7
Paperback ISBN 978-1-60684-230-0

Book design by Jeanine Henderson

Printed in the United States of America

For Rob

1
A Visitor

The man in the stained suit stared up at the driveway that ended at Thomas Edison's Victorian mansion. He'd sworn to himself that this day would never come—when he'd have to grovel like a dog at the feet of his old enemy. But news of the famous scientist's declining health had reached Manhattan, and the man had one final score to settle with his old rival.

Trudging toward the door, he winced as tiny pebbles pierced his worn-out soles. He desperately needed new shoes, but every cent he earned went toward rent. Twelve dollars a month for one shabby room and hot plate—criminal! A sorry end for the man who helped invent the X-ray and radio, who had once been offered $150,000 by J.P. Morgan himself to redesign the entire Niagara Falls Power Plant.

The maid answered on the first ring.

"I'm here to see Thomas Edison." Even in front of this servant, he was self-conscious about his patched jacket and uncombed hair.

"I'm afraid Mr. Edison isn't seeing any more visitors."

"Tell him it's his old colleague, Nikola Tesla." As the words left his mouth, the maid seemed to catch her breath.

"This way," she murmured, smoothing her apron, then leading him through the foyer and up the creaky stairs.

Entering the bedroom, Tesla immediately sensed the contempt of the others who were already gathered to pay their respects. He had not expected to see them, and his stomach churned with each recognizable face: Babe Ruth, Harvey Firestone, Henry Ford—even the silvery-haired New York Governor Franklin Roosevelt had taken a break from his presidential campaign to make the trip to New Jersey. They were Edison's inner circle, and once upon a time, Tesla had considered a few of them his dear friends and colleagues. Now mistrust and betrayal had distanced them.

Propped up by pillows, his old rival regarded him with those same electric blue eyes. Tesla could feel the edges of his heart soften. If he'd had a hat, he'd have removed it. Respect trumped dislike, even now.

"How many years has it been, Nikola?" Edison finally spoke. His voice was weak and raspy.

"Ten, twelve?" Tesla was shocked at how frail the inventor had become. As young scientists, the two of them had been tireless, working straight through the night, fueled by nothing more than the excitement of discovery.

He cleared his throat. "Thomas, could I have a moment in private?"

Edison gave a knowing nod, then signaled for the others to take their reluctant leave.

"They hate me," said Tesla as soon as the group had vacated the room.

"They fear you."

Ha! This, from the man who ruined my career. "I assume you know why I've come," said Tesla.

Edison closed his eyes and nodded. His expression was one of resigned irritation.

Even now, at death's doorstep, the old man is still so condescending, Tesla thought.

He could feel the angry blood rushing to his head like hot lava.

"Give me the formula!" he shouted into the silence. He hadn't meant to blurt it out like that, but old wounds had been torn open.

"You are much too angry to be trusted—"

"Your opinion is not my concern. You stole my research, then destroyed my life's work."

Edison began to cough. Tesla automatically reached for the pitcher of water by his bed and poured a glass, then handed it to him.

"You still wear that stupid ring," Tesla noted when he saw the aged scientist's hand. A single emerald set within filigree gold adorned his pinkie. "Just to rub it in my face."

"Whatever actions I've taken in my life were done for a reason," said Edison. "And whatever emotional burdens I carry are mine alone."

"You had no right to do what you did! So let's just finish this business, and I'll be on my way."

"I don't know what you're talking about." Edison glanced toward the open window, unable to look his old colleague in the eyes. Lying had never been one of the inventor's strong suits.

"You know I have as much right to it as anyone else!" Tesla added, "Even more."

"There are rumors that you roam the Bowery," said Edison after a moment, with slow care to his words, "addled with drink, cursing my name. And now that I see you, I know the worst."

It was Tesla's turn to be silent. He shifted his weight, embarrassed.

"You have lost your mind, my friend," said Edison, his tone softening now. "To give you any power at all would be unconscionable."

"You are not God!" And before he could make full sense of his actions, Tesla had lifted the water pitcher and, in a burst of fury, sent it crashing to the floor, a smash of icy water and splintering shards.

"Get out! You foolish man!" Henry Ford's voice was like a knife to the back. Tesla spun to see Ford and Firestone barreling through the door toward him, and before Tesla could protest, Harvey had him by the lapels and was pushing him into the hallway.

"This isn't over!" Tesla heard himself yell, like a spurned villain from one of those new Buck Rogers comic strips, as he was shoved down the stairs and out the front door so quickly it left him gasping for breath.

He was alone now; his trousers were soaked from the smashed water pitcher. Bits of glass clung to them, reflecting a kaleidoscope prism of light. He blinked, a moment's pause at the unexpected beauty. He'd spent his life working in spectrums of light, sound, and energy. So brilliant, so marvelous, so many years ago.

And now only one thought filled his head, a truth as unforgiving and absolute as the cold winter sun. If he wanted to claim his formula—the formula for turning base metal into pure gold—he would have to fight for it.

2
Clorox Invention #28

"I'm about to make you a legend, Noodle."

Tom Edison IV's unruly tuft of blond bed hair stuck out from behind the wood-framed car as his thin fingers nimbly connected an eight-volt battery to a large bundle of wires. "We're both going down in history with this one."

Why did Tom always make things a billion times crazier than they had to be? thought Bernard—aka Noodle—Zuckerberg to himself. None of the other ten soapbox cars at the starting line even had motors.

Noodle tried to calm his nerves by focusing on the thumping rap beats pulsing through the iPod earbuds hidden beneath his scribbly hair, but it wasn't helping. At five feet, ten inches—by far the gangliest in his class—he looked and felt like an oversize giraffe test-driving a Prius.

His knobby knees stuck out the side of the car, and he had to hunch his body just to fit inside this mobile death trap. No wonder people had been calling him Noodle since his first day at Saint Vincent's.

"And you're sure this thing's one hundred percent safe?" he yelled over the music while bopping his head along to the beat.

"Of course it's safe," Tom said confidently as he peeked his freckled face around the side of the car, although the truth was, he'd never exactly tested the design for the bleach-battery motor he and his dad had formulated exactly three weekends ago in their basement lab.

Tom pulled the engine's rope, and the car coughed to life. Black smoke billowed into the air as every other kid in Mr. Fazool's science class gaped.

"All right, my little Jeff Gordons, remember—today's race isn't about winning." Fifty yards away, at the other end of the parking lot, Tom's shaggy-haired science teacher, Mr. Fazool, fiddled with the cap gun. "It's about . . . er, observing the concepts we studied this semester. Kinetic and potential energy, friction . . ."

All month long, the seventh graders at Saint Vincent's

had been working on their cars, sawing down blocks of wood and fastening on plastic wheels, while Tom feverishly constructed his latest invention like a mad scientist.

"Ten bucks that beast stalls right out of the gates." Strapped into the triple-reinforced car next to theirs sat brown-haired, pigtailed Colby McCracken, Tom's only other friend in class, beaming at him.

"Not a chance, Colb," Tom fired back. "Prepare to be blown out of the water."

"You're way too ADD to pull it off," she said. "I'm sure you messed up the calculations along the way."

Maybe Tom wasn't the math whiz Colby was—he was more of a big-ideas guy—but he had ambition. And he knew a bleach-powered electric car would be as revolutionary as his great-great-grandfather's first commercial lightbulb.

"On your mark. Get set—"

Bang! As Mr. Fazool fired the gun early, Noodle's startled foot hit the pedal, blasting his car to life. Its axles glittered against the pavement.

"Ease the brake!" Tom shouted. "You gotta slow down!"

"Yo, I did! I can't!" Noodle's voice echoed as the car

whizzed down the parking lot, making windy tracks of burned rubber behind it.

Tom darted after him. What was going wrong? Maybe he should have added more sugar? Or maybe the bleach ionized too quickly?

Either way, that car was moving way too fast.

"Noodle!" he shouted, racing after his now smoking creation. "Stay calm!"

"Tom, you promised me no more malfunctions!" Mr. Fazool had dropped his clipboard and had joined the footrace to catch Noodle.

Up ahead, a school bus turned a corner and was beginning to veer straight into Noodle's path. Tom could see his friend's elbows madly jerking the wheel left and right, but the car maintained a direct crash course toward the bus.

Hoooooooonk! The bus belched its warning as Noodle narrowly whizzed past its front bumper. The car had a mind of its own now, wheeling past a cluster of gossiping sophomores, then heading directly toward the middle of the campus quad.

"Watch it!"

"Slow down!"

"Sorry!" Noodle's voice was pure fear.

His heart thudding, Tom pumped his legs faster to keep up with the car, which had bumped up onto the sidewalk, and was now fast-approaching a long flight of stairs that led down to the upper school gym. He could barely watch as the car hit the stairs and began tearing down them, heading straight into the pride of the Saint Vincent's Academy campus, its reservoir.

Which was centered by a stone fountain statue of old Saint Vincent himself.

Kids were shrieking and whooping, their phones out to snap pictures, though it was all Tom could do not to hide his eyes as . . . *splash!*

Nose first, Noodle second, the car hit and then submerged, displacing a wave of water that soaked over the lip of the reservoir and onto the quad lawn.

A hiss, and then, silence. All eyes, even the stony downcast eyes of Saint Vincent, watched Tom's latest bright idea as it sank.

"Someone needs to jump in."

"I think that dude might be drowning."

More students gathered around. Nobody was snapping pictures anymore.

"Coming through!" Tom yelled, pushing into the

crowd. "Outta my way!" Memories of learning mouth-to-mouth at the Y catapulted through his brain. If anything happened to Noodle, he would never be able to live with himself. He dove in—just as his friend wobbled and sputtered to the water's surface, looking like a wet poodle.

"He lives!" Some kids burst into applause, while others shook their heads, as Tom and Noodle, soaked and somber, climbed out of the water.

"I'm not sure we're going down in history," said Noodle when he saw their breathless and angry science teacher approaching. "But I sure think we're going down to see Phelps."

"Hey, Edison," yelled a blond-haired senior from behind them. Tom turned around and met his smirking face. "Is there anything you don't screw up?"

3
In Trouble, Again

It was not an ideal way to end the last day before spring break.

Sitting in Headmaster Phelps's wood-paneled, leather-smelling office on a Thursday afternoon, Tom chewed his fingernails down to the nubs. Partly from nerves, but also because he was one of those fidgety kids who couldn't sit still for longer than two-minute intervals. Even when he was in trouble, his mind was a distracted flurry of explosions and ideas. This was probably the reason he'd been summoned to this very office three times in just as many months.

Experience had taught Tom that the best thing to do when being lectured was to stare straight ahead with an appropriately remorseful look on his face, and at all costs avoid eye contact with his no-nonsense mother, who'd been called out of Highland Elementary, where she'd been substitute teaching.

Last time he had gotten into this kind of trouble, Phelps had threatened to take away his scholarship. Then, Tom had sworn to his parents—and truly believed—that he was turning over a new leaf and that his days of detentions were over.

How had he managed to mess up so spectacularly? Again?

"Steven, you've known Tom since he was in first grade." His mom tried her best to sound composed as she attempted to placate the quietly smoldering Dr. Phelps. Tom knew it was going to be a far less diplomatic conversation once they got home. "He's always cooking up his little inventions—"

"Little inventions? June, you're a teacher. Don't pull the wool over your own eyes. Your son's out of control. Just last week, he invented a way to destroy half the football field."

Tom piped up in his own defense. "That's a quick fix. All those mowers need is a GPS installed, and they'll—"

"And how would you 'quick-fix' your bionic lunch

lady?" The angry blue vein pulsing on the side of Dr. Phelps's head was a good indication for Tom to keep his mouth shut. So he did.

Phelps just didn't get it. Once Tom had ironed out all the kinks in those auto-mowers, he knew he could save the maintenance staff hours of labor on a sweltering hot day.

And then, he'd be a legend.

"This is your third strike, Tom." Phelps held up three chubby fingers to clarify. "So I want you to use this spring break to mull over a better academic fit. Maybe take a tour of Astoria Junior High, what do you think?"

Tom saw the panic flicker in his mom's eyes. "But Tom is the third generation of Edisons to go to Saint Vincent's," she protested. "Our family name has always—"

"Frankly, June, the Edison name, such that it is, is not what it was."

Tom bit hard on his tongue. It was bad enough when kids at school teased him for not having the Edison gene every time one of his inventions went spastic, but now his own principal thought he was a loser.

Dr. Phelps stood up from behind his desk. "I'm very sorry, but I'm handing the matter over to the academic policy board. We'll let you know if we think Tom should be allowed to return to Saint Vincent's after spring break."

"Well, it might not even matter anyway," said his mom on her way out of the office, though Tom wasn't sure exactly what she meant by that.

4
More Bad News

A rright, invention number five-one-six. Do not fail me." It was later that evening, and Tom was back to the drawing board. He usually found the best cure for a bad day was losing himself in a new project.

Working quickly, he hooked the robot's CD-player body to its spatula arm. His latest project, Nanny Golightly, was a huge improvement on his auto-mowers, and potentially the invention to put the Edison family back on the map.

Once Toys "R" Us bought the prototype, Tom was planning to take everyone—Noodle, Colby, his parents, and his little sister—on an all-expense-paid trip to Switzerland, where all the coolest stuff had been invented.

Everything from the electronic wristwatch to the computer mouse to Ovaltine!

"Naa gooo righh!" Tom's three-year-old sister, Rose, cheered him on from the corner of his room, where she liked to craft her own creations out of building blocks and dismembered doll parts.

Downstairs, he heard the sound of his father opening the front door.

"Time for me to pay the piper, Rosie." Tom dropped his wrench, then tiptoed to the top of the stairs. If he could hear his parents' conversation first, he'd be better prepared for the talking-to that would definitely be coming his way later.

"So?" His mother's voice. Nervous.

"It's official. They laid off my division this morning." *Uh-oh.* Job conversations were tense business in the Edison household these days. Tom's dad had been working for Alset Energy's Bronx plant as a mechanical engineer for more than ten years, but over the past few months Curt Keller, its CEO, had been cutting people's jobs right and left. It was an unfair policy, picketers cried, and all because Keller had failed to pay fines for loads of infractions against the Clean Air Act.

"Well, it's not like we didn't see it coming," said his mother. "You officially said yes?"

Yes? Yes to what? Tom leaned farther over the banister to listen.

"My first day's in two weeks." Aha. His dad must've gotten a new job. That was potentially good news. Maybe they'd all go out and celebrate at Giovanni's and forget all about Tom's trip to the principal's office.

"Tom's up in his room. We had a run-in with Phelps this afternoon. Third strike, if you're counting." No luck. He could always count on his mom to cut right to the bad news. She was the family's anchor, while Tom and his dad usually kept their heads above the clouds.

"Not sure it matters," said his father. "Given the circumstances."

Given what circumstances? Tom thought. Their conversation was growing more confusing by the second. He was more than happy to skip his punishment, but something about his dad's weary tone made him nervous.

"I'd better go up and deliver the news." As soon as Tom heard his dad scuffling toward the stairs, he darted back into his room and jumped onto the bed, grabbing the latest issue of *Popular Mechanics*.

"Hey." The glint from his dad's glasses peeked through the door crack.

"What's going on?" Tom looked up from his magazine as his dad did his usual trick of knocking while entering.

"Daddeeeeee!" squealed Rose.

"Another pen explosion?" Tom nodded to the blooming black ink spot on his father's fraying shirt. At least once a week he'd come home from work with a new mystery stain—grease, mustard, even the rare chemical burn mark.

"Oh yeah—that." His dad smoothed over the stain, a little embarrassed. "Must've happened sometime between lunch and when I got on the train home."

Tom rolled his eyes as his dad took a seat at the edge of the bed and swung Rose into his lap. "Sooo—I have some interesting news for you both," he said. "I got a new job."

"That R and D one in South Orange?" Tom had overheard his parents the other day talking about a couple prospects in New Jersey.

"Nope. No R and D for me. My title, actually"—his dad tried for a chuckle—"is Waste Engineer. And it's not as much pay as Alset. But the good news is . . . it's not anywhere we've been before. It's a whole new adventure for us. In Wichita."

20

Good news? Tom wondered if it was possible to mathematically calculate the direct relationship between the badness of the news and the forced wideness of his dad's smile.

"The same Wichita that's in Kansas?" Maybe there was a very charming Wichita Street in Yonkers, only a few minutes' bike ride from Noodle's and Colby's houses.

"The Wichita where that meteor fell." Tom's mother had suddenly materialized in the doorway. "Near Dorothy and Toto, too," she added for Rosie's benefit.

No, no, no. This was not a joke. Tom looked from his father's face to his mother's. He could feel himself starting to panic. They couldn't move. His whole life was in New York. And then out of the corner of his eye, he saw the answer to their problems . . . Nanny Golightly. *Aha!* It was a little early for the unveiling, but the prototype was basically finished.

He swung his legs off the bed.

"Mom, Dad—we don't need to go to Wichita. Once I sell the patent for Nanny Golightly, we won't have to go anywhere. We'll be loaded."

"Nanny Go-who?" His dad, who loved anything to do with gadgets, patents, and inventions, couldn't help but look curious.

His mother, however, was already shaking her head. "Tom, don't make this situation worse. We need to be realistic right now."

But Tom only had eyes for the invention that would save them all. He placed a picture book into one of Nanny's oven-mitt hands, then pressed play on the CD player. "Mom, remember how you were saying you never get enough time to read to Rosie?"

"Look, honey, you can still see Noodle and Colby in the summer," said his mother, not really listening. "They can visit—"

"Well, now you can!" Tom interrupted. "Because I recorded three hours of you singing to her, then burned it onto a CD. Six songs, including her favorite, 'She'll Be Coming 'Round the Mountain.'"

"Roun mountay!" Rose clapped her hands, recognizing the title.

"See? Already got a request." And before anyone could utter another word, the sound of his mom's voice piped sweetly out of Nanny Golightly's microphone mouthpiece. *She'll be coming 'round the mountain when she comes—*

"Roun moun..." Rose was all dimpled grin. His

mother even looked warily impressed as the robot's mismatched arms turned pages in time with her singing.

"You just plop your kid down in front of the robot here," Tom boasted like a used-car salesman, "and let Nanny Golightly here do the rest!"

"A little WD-40 through the shoulder hinges there'd do wonders," pointed out his father, his spirits momentarily lifted.

"Great idea, Dad." Tom was beaming. "Love the enthusiasm."

This is it, he couldn't help thinking. It was destiny. Ninety-nine percent perspiration had finally paid off. The Edison family wasn't moving anywhere.

"She'll be coming 'round the mountain, she'll be coming 'round the mountain." Abruptly, Nanny's voice lurched into a Darth Vader bass tone, her arms slowing down. In the next second she sped up, her tin voice now squeaking like a chipmunk's.

Smack! The malfunctioning robot hurled the picture book across the room.

Rose began to cry.

"Tom! Please stop that thing!" His mother scooped up his baby sister from her father's lap, as Tom jiggered with

Nanny's buttons and gadget appendages. Too late. With a hollow pop, Nanny's head sprang off her body and flew into the air.

Rose immediately stopped crying, so shocked and frightened she could not make a peep.

"It's all right, sweetheart." Hoisting Rose over her shoulder, Tom's mother hurried from the room. "Just another one of your brother's crazy inventions."

Alone now, Tom and his dad remained silent, staring down at Nanny's decapitated head.

Disappointment crushed Tom like a boulder. So close, so close.

"Right." His father cleared his throat. "As I was saying, there's lots of cool things in Wichita. You'll see—"

"But Dad, what about our other inventions? Like the Clorox battery? I tested it today, and except for a few little kinks—"

"Son." Mr. Edison raised a weary hand. "Our weekend projects are fun, and a wonderful way to spend time together, but this is life. And in life, there's a time when I have to realize who I am ... and what I'm not."

"But you can't give up! You're the best inventor I know!" Tom was on his feet. His mom was a lost cause, but if he could just get through to his dad, maybe there was still hope for the family. "There's gotta be loads of other jobs here," Tom continued. His eyes were getting wet and stingy at the edges. "We could start our own invention business."

"Son—"

"I'll quit school and devote myself full-time to—"

"*Son!*"

Tom's mouth snapped shut. He couldn't remember the last time his father had ever raised his voice. "Inventions don't pay the bills. At least mine don't. Right now, I need to do what's best for this family."

"But if we worked together—"

"End of discussion," said his dad, cutting him off. "We all need to make the best of this situation. For each other."

Tom stayed silent and kept his eyes fixed on Nanny's dinged head, until his father left the bedroom.

Sitting there on the floor, he came to a sad realization.

This was the worst day of his life.

5
Hidden Heirloom

Tom's basement laboratory consisted of one crooked card table pushed into a dark corner next to the washing machine. His work space and the shelves above it were crammed with books, tools, thingamajigs, and defunct inventions of Edisons past and present: stock ticker, phonograph, and a framed old photograph of Tom's famous double-great-grandfather or T.E. 1, as the family sometimes referred to him.

"Why does nothing in my life ever work?" Tom asked the unresponsive photo.

He had devoured so many biographies of Thomas Edison, however, and knew enough family lore to imagine exactly how his double-great would've answered.

Something along the lines of, *Discontent is the first necessity of progress,* or the old guy's favorite gem, *Just because something doesn't do what you planned it to do doesn't mean it's useless.*

Tom liked to have pretend conversations with T.E. 1. while he worked. It made him feel like he wasn't alone in his quests and kept him from ever feeling too sorry for himself. Like when Edison was Tom's age, for example, he got scarlet fever and lost most of his hearing. That was probably as bad as moving to Kansas.

Everything that had happened the day before—Wichita, the runaway car, Wichita, Dr. Phelps, the failure of his last two inventions, Wichita—all melted away as Tom fell into work. Reassembling Nanny had been the only thing he wanted to do since he'd woken up on this first official morning of spring break.

She was his only chance, he was sure, to keep the family put and restore the Edison name.

"All right, Nanny, expect some minor discomfort here." Tom yanked a thin copper wire from the robot's broken glass eye, which he'd originally swiped from an old telescope. Scanning the shelves and tables for a replacement, his own eyes zoomed in on a dusty science-kit telescope, balanced precariously on the very top of the bookshelf. Its dusty lens was calling to him.

"Sweet. Nanny, ole girl, time to meet your new eye-ball."

Tom hopped onto one of the lower shelves and felt it tremble under his weight. Then, before really weighing the pros and cons of the idea, he hoisted himself up another wobbly shelf, which groaned under the strain. His fingertips pawed the air, then batted the telescope, shifting it even closer to the ledge.

The bookcase teetered.

Tap-tap-tap! Noodle's and Colby's faces had appeared at the sooty basement window, and as Tom looked over, he lost his balance, which sent the entire bookcase, loaded with tons of antique machines, toppling down on him.

"Argh!" Tom covered his head and in the last split second rolled out of the way, right before the splintering, deafening, resounding crash.

"Tom?" his dad called from upstairs.

"Are you all right?" his mom shouted, just as worried, plus 10 percent more.

"I'm fine!"

"What'd you break?" Dad called again.

"Nothing. Everything's under control. No need to come down." Gasping, Tom peered up at the window, but Noodle and Colby were gone. Seconds later, he heard a clamoring of footsteps above him, then the basement door swung open, and they came barreling down the stairs.

"What a mess!" said Noodle. "Looks like a land mine went off in here."

Tom rolled onto his side and came face-to-face with an antique Leica 35-millimeter camera that had fallen to the floor. A brand-new hairline crack ran down its middle. Tom could tell from its casing and adjustment knobs that the thing must have been at least seventy or eighty years old.

"Perfect," he said, studying the newly broken antique. "There goes my allowance for the year." How was he going to break it to his parents that on top of everything else, he'd also destroyed a family heirloom?

Colby glanced around the room, surveying the destruction, then reached into her pocket and snuck a quick puff off her always-present inhaler.

"Aren't you a little old for fake asthma attacks, Colb?" Noodle teased.

"Tom just unleashed about six million species of dust mites in here." She added an extra-phlegm-filled cough to prove her point. Since birth, Colb's nana had instilled in her an intense fear of anything airborne and potentially disease causing.

"Yo, lemme see that beast." Noodle snatched the broken camera out of Tom's hands and examined its lens and levers. "Sure woulda been tough to be the paparazzi back in the eighteen nineties, huh?" He side stepped past Tom, pretending to fire off glamour shots of Colby. "Hold that pose, babe. Just four more minutes. Yer byootiful!"

"The thirty-five millimeter wasn't even invented until nineteen fourteen," corrected Tom.

"Why do you know that?"

In an answer, Tom lunged for the camera, but Noodle was too quick. And with a full four-inch height advantage, he could keep it well out of reach. Tom's final shove knocked the instrument out of Noodle's hand, though, and as it crashed to the floor, a two-inch-long paper-covered spool popped out of a spring compartment in the back.

The mysterious cylinder hit the floor and rolled under the card table.

"Whoa! What was that?" Thanks to six years of

gymnastics classes, Colby effortlessly leaped over the fallen bookshelf, then stretched herself low, between the wall and Tom's work table, to scoop up the fallen cylinder.

Tom and Noodle gathered around her as she unrolled the curl of yellowed paper, brittle as a wood shaving, that was wrapped around it.

"It's a roll of film!" Tom could hardly believe it. All this time the camera had just been sitting there on his bookshelf, and he'd never even thought to look inside. His mind raced as he tried to imagine what these priceless, undeveloped photographs could be of—Thomas Edison's Menlo Park lab? An unknown invention?

"There's some writing." Colby squinted as Noodle and Tom jockeyed for a better view of the handwritten note. The letters were cryptic and delicate, as if they'd been scripted with an old feather quill.

"'*When you reach the Bed, Ford. You're just one hundred yards north of the sun and moon,*'" she read.

"Think it's from the real Thomas Edison?" Noodle wondered aloud.

"Hey, I'm also the real—"

"You know what I mean. The famous one."

"Who's Ford? Like Henry Ford?" Colby was biting her

lip the way she always did just before she called out the right answer to a math problem at school.

Beneath the riddle was stamped the print of a rose inside a perfect, thin circle. Tom plucked the roll of film from Colby's fingers.

"I wonder how old it is." He felt the urge to add that roll film was invented by a farmer in Wisconsin named David Houston, but thought better of it, since Noodle would definitely make fun of him for that tidbit.

"I bet you it's pictures of scary dead people." Noodle's eyes were alive with anticipation.

"Uh, Dad?" Tom called up to the kitchen. "Can you come down here and promise you won't yell about the mess?"

For right now, Nanny Golightly would have to wait.

6
Polished Silver

"So this isn't the kind of film you take to a Rite Aid and get back in an hour, is it?" Tom stared up at his dad, who was holding the stiff scrap of paper half an inch from his thick-lensed glasses as he inspected the encircled rose beneath the riddle.

"No, but photographs are nothing more than silver oxide," he answered, though his thoughts seemed to be somewhere else.

"And how does that help us, Big T?" said Noodle.

"Developing them's not all that different from polishing a tarnished set of knives and forks."

"So we're gonna polish the photos?" asked Colby.

"Sort of." Tom's dad began sifting through his messy workspace, grabbing a few plastic canisters. "This really is

33

something," he added as he bent down to search through a lower cabinet of grimy, unlabeled plastic bottles. Thankfully, he'd been so fascinated by the roll of film and riddle that he wasn't too upset about the fallen bookcase. Tom's mom, on the other hand, would be a different story.

"What are you looking for?" Tom asked.

"Sodium bicarbonate, among other things. I thought we had some around here." After a few more minutes of rummaging, Tom's dad headed toward the basement's old, rusty fridge. "We'll just have to improvise with the old beer-and-baking-soda recipe. Chemically speaking, it's the same as any low-acid film developer."

At that moment, Tom couldn't understand how his dad could settle for life as a waste engineer. The guy was easily the smartest person Tom had ever met, and it killed him to think of his father being bossed around at yet another dead-end job when he could be changing the world with his inventions.

What was it about being an Edison? Were they just cursed with bad luck?

His dad returned to the worktable holding a just-opened beer can that looked like it had been bought during the Great Depression, then expertly mixed it in with one of the solutions.

"Tom, measure me out a half cup of baking soda." His dad was pointing and snapping his fingers like an air traffic control man as he carefully poured several more mixtures into various Tupperware containers. "Colby, find some clothespins for the negatives. When they're ready, we'll need to transfer them to someplace dark quickly."

"How about letting me polish off that brew dog?" asked Noodle.

"How about finding me a couple beakers for these photo baths?" Tom's dad answered, then placed the roll of film into a plastic, solution-filled container.

"Lame!" Noodle stomped off in search of the beakers. He was the only one who could get away with being a smart aleck to Tom's parents, since he'd been a staple at their house since kindergarten.

"If it's pictures of the Loch Ness monster or something good, I want a cut," Colby joked as the four of them continued readying the materials.

Everyone went quiet while Tom's dad washed the film, then plopped it into the developing solution. Once it had dried, faint grainy outlines began to take shape.

"Yo, there is definitely something on that film." Noodle began to hop around. "The suspense is killing me."

"But it looks like only one photo was taken," Tom noted. "In the whole roll."

"Get comfortable," said Mr. Edison as he removed the negative and clipped it to a clothesline. "'Cause this is going to take another hour. At least."

7

Key to the Past

nd once I'd paid for NYU drama school and Kanye's producing fees on my demo, if there was any cash left, I'd build myself an in-home recording studio." Noodle leaned back with his hands behind his head, quite pleased with his answer. "Okay, your turn," he said with a nod toward Colby.

"I'd probably buy a beachfront house somewhere along the Jersey shore for me and Nana."

For the last hour, they'd been in Tom's room playing the game "What's the First Thing You'd Do If These Photos End Up Being Worth Ten Million Dollars?"

Tom knew exactly what he'd do with the money: give it to his parents so they wouldn't have to move. He didn't say that out loud, though, because one, that was a super-boring answer, and two, he was nowhere near ready to drop that bomb on Noodle and Colb. The three of them had been an unbreakable posse ever since he could remember. How many kids got to have their two best (and only) friends at school live within a three-block radius? Tom's life without them was too depressing to even contemplate.

"I would have hated olden times," sighed Noodle as he fell face-first onto Tom's bed. "Everything was one long wait. Like dial-up."

"And then you died of something painful and undiagnosed," added Colby. "Like scurvy or rickets."

"I don't think you die from rickets," Tom chimed in.

"You really need to chill with your hypochondria issues, Colb," said Noodle. "It was cute when we were eight, but that sorta drama won't fly in high school. I'll have to pretend not to know you." Again, Tom tried not to think about Noodle and Colby in high school without him.

"It's not half as lame as being obsessed with comic books," she fired back.

"I'm a collector! It's an investment."

"Kids!" Tom's dad's voice called up to them from downstairs.

"They're ready!" Tom shouted as the three of them tore down the stairs into the basement, where his dad was holding a glass photo loop against the one developed negative. Each of the kids then took turns looking through the lens at the magnified image of a thin-faced, gray-haired man seated in a brick-walled study.

"None of the other exposures look like they were used," Tom's dad said.

"It's definitely not your double-great," said Colby. "This guy looks more like an aging movie star."

"I bet you anything it's an old Charlie Chaplin," joked Noodle.

"It's Harvey Firestone," said Tom's dad. "He was one of Edison's best friends."

"The tire guy?" Tom could barely contain his excitement.

"Uh-huh. Edison, Ford, and Firestone were known as the fathers of modernity."

"This could be worth some real dough then," said Noodle.

"Doubtful," Tom's dad answered. "We had a few photos from the attic appraised a while back. It's probably worth a couple hundred dollars."

Tom's heart sank. He'd been secretly hoping for more. A lot more.

"But what about the riddle?" asked Colby, scanning the paper that was pronged in her fingers.

"Uh, I'm not sure what to make of that." Tom's dad averted his eyes. "I don't think it's too important either." None of the Edison men were good liars, and Tom couldn't help wondering what his dad might be hiding. There was something forced about his casual tone.

"Make sure you hit the lights on your way up," Mr. Edison said as he climbed the stairs with the Firestone negative in his hands.

Despite the disappointment, Tom still felt like he'd been meant to find that photo. Like it was his destiny.

The question was, why?

8
Golden Cookbook

Tom, Noodle, and Colby had decided the best way to celebrate the first night of spring break was with a sleepover, though it was almost midnight, and the three of them weren't doing much sleeping.

Once his parents had gone to bed, Tom had tiptoed into his dad's study and swiped the Firestone negative, which he'd been examining intently with the magnifying lens for almost an hour.

Up close, he could see that Firestone's hand was resting on a leather-bound book, and his index finger was pointing toward something Tom could not see. Embossed on the book's spine was a title, *The Alchemy Treatise*, which Tom could barely make out, and the wood beams running along the ceiling behind Firestone were intricately carved and painted with fleurs-de-lis and various family shields. The window over his left shoulder looked out onto an old-fashioned city landscape, where the distinct curved edge of a tall brick building was just visible.

"I got something here." Noodle's face popped up from behind his laptop, where he'd been doing some online research on *The Alchemy Treatise*. "It says this book was some kind of recipe manual from the Middle Ages."

"For what?" said Colby. "Making fish soup and weird serf food?"

"No, it's for, like, people who wanna turn base metals into gold." Tom and Colby went silent. "Apparently, this alchemy stuff was all the rage back then."

"So maybe Firestone and my double-great were into, like, medieval witchcraft," said Tom.

"Maybe they were the original Dungeons and Dragons geeks."

"I haven't even told you the good part yet," interrupted Noodle. "Six copies of *The Alchemy Treatise* are left in existence. And one of them"—he let his words linger, drawing out the suspense like he was telling a ghost story at a campfire—"is at the Met."

Only an hour away by train.

Of all the places in the world, Tom thought. *This book's just a few miles from my house.* Destiny was calling to him louder than ever.

"I think this is a clue," he announced to them after a moment.

"For what?" said Colby.

"I have no idea. But think about it. There's that weird riddle about the sun and moon. And only one photo was taken? In the entire roll? Don't you find that sorta strange?"

"Seems like a stretch," said Noodle. "Plus your dad said the riddle meant nothing."

"Yeah, that's another piece. Didn't you guys think my dad was acting weird about this whole thing?"

Colby and Noodle shook their heads no, but Tom was on his feet now, pacing.

"You said it yourself, Noodle. *The Alchemy Treatise* is a recipe book for making gold. Maybe there's some kinda gold treasure hidden somewhere. And this book's the next clue."

"Not sure I'm buying all that, but I guess the book's worth checking out," said Noodle after a moment. "You got me sorta curious about it now."

"Are you two out of your freaking minds?" Colby was looking back and forth between Tom and Noodle. "There's no treasure. It's just a photo and a dumb riddle. That's it."

"Colb, we're a crew. This is what we do," said Noodle. "Tom's the crazy daredevil. You're the levelheaded brainiac. And I'm . . . the smooth operator."

"No, you're the idiot." Colby was shaking her head. "This is how you guys always get me in trouble. With your stupid schemes."

"It's spring break. What else are we gonna do?" said Noodle.

Colby raised her hands. "Look, it doesn't matter. I know I'm never going to convince you this is a dumb plan, so I might as well just save myself the headache and go along with it."

"So you'll come with us?" asked Tom.

Colby rolled her eyes. "Yes, but that's it!"

It was settled. The three would head to the museum tomorrow on a preliminary recon mission. Without Tom's dad.

As Tom crept back into his father's study, he realized that slight nagging feeling had grown into a riptide pull.

Every slight against his family name, every lost job, every failed invention, it all bubbled over onto that Firestone photo. Tom was meant to find this clue. He was sure of it. And he was going to do whatever it took to unlock its secrets and prove to the world that the Edison name was not a punch line but a badge of honor.

And so, the trio was once again off on a new adventure. Tom prayed it would not be their last.

9
The Secret Exhibit

Y our timing is quite terrible, you know," muttered the wizened gremlin of a curator as he led Tom, Noodle, and Colby through a room of Italian Renaissance paintings. "The Science and Mysticism exhibit doesn't open until next month."

The curator waved his magnetic ID badge in front of a glass door, which unlocked it.

"Whoa," said Noodle as they followed him into the dark exhibit. "Do you ever feel like you're the commander of the starship *Enterprise*?"

"Sometimes." The curator chuckled.

Tom was thankful he had Noodle. The kid could charm a troll, and the term *off-limits* simply wasn't in his vocabulary. At first, the curator had been less than thrilled to let three seventh graders into a closed exhibit. That was, until Noodle went into a long-winded story about their extra-credit history project on medieval sorcery, peppering in heart-wrenching details about how it had been his great-grandfather's dying wish to see a copy of *The Alchemy Treatise* in person, as well as Noodle's own life-changing field trip to Sir Isaac Newton's alchemy lab in England. None of it was true, of course. But it got them access to—

"The Curt Keller exhibit." Colby read the name off a metal placard affixed to the entrance archway. Tom's neck hairs prickled at the name. Curt Keller? Could it be the same Curt Keller who'd just laid off his father? The man who was responsible for his family's move?

Inside, the exhibit was incredible. Gold-painted star maps covered the walls, and glass cases displayed manuscripts and illustrated texts from all over the world. It was hard to miss the overriding theme of this exhibit. Most of the precious objects were related to one thing—alchemy. There were oil paintings of dour alchemists in their labs, plus a group of shelves filled with golden weighing scales and antique vials used for distilling liquids.

"Do all these pieces belong to Mr. Keller?" Tom asked.

"Most of them," said the curator. "His interest in the occult is widely known. And he's especially fascinated by alchemy. Much like yourself, Mr. Zuckerberg."

"I'd like to meet this Mr. Keller," said Noodle, surveying the room with a scholar's seriousness.

And then Tom saw what they had come here for, open and displayed inside its own sealed glass case—*The Alchemy Treatise*. So stunning, it almost made him swallow his gum. Its pages were razor thin, its edges dipped in gold leaf, and lavish paintings of astrological imagery adorned the borders of its calligraphy text.

Tom touched his nose to the glass. His fingers itched to turn a page.

"Hands to yourself!" the curator loudly reminded him from across the room. "That's a five-hundred-year-old artifact."

"Er, sorry." He jammed his hands back into his pockets.

Mouth twitching in suspicion, the curator glided a

little closer to Tom to give him a quick once-over.

"Tom, I think I found something," whispered Colby as she tugged on his sleeve and nodded toward the adjoining room. Her eyes were alive with excitement. "You'll definitely want to see this."

10
Sign of the Rose

I t was an oil painting of a well-known mustached politi-
cian hanging on the far wall of the room. The plaque
next to it read: PORTRAIT OF THEODORE ROOSEVELT,
1915.

"It's a painting of Teddy Roosevelt, Colb. Big deal.
There's probably a million of them."

"The question is what it's doing in an exhibit on science
and mysticism," she whispered with a glance toward the
unsuspecting curator. "Look closer."

Tom followed her finger, which pointed to the familiar
circled rose symbol—the same one that had been stamped
beneath the camera's riddle had also been painted in red
strokes just above the artist's signature.

"It's gotta be connected to the photo somehow," Tom

whispered back. He was getting that all-too-familiar butterfly feeling, the same one he got when he was close to an experimental breakthrough. "We need to know if this symbol is anywhere in *The Alchemy Treatise*."

"Salvatore?" squawked the walkie-talkie that was hooked to the curator's belt.

"Yes, Amanda?" he answered.

"Buford Bixby is in the foyer."

"Tell him I'll be right down." Salvatore approached Tom and Colby with his hands clasped behind his back and a phony smile plastered to his face. "I'm afraid our time is up, kids."

Tom shot a pleading glance toward Noodle. *Work your magic.*

"Five more minutes?" said Noodle, picking up his cue as he approached the curator from behind. "Please? My great-grandfather would've wanted that."

"I'm terribly sorry, but I've already broken enough museum regulations for one day. And the exhibit will be open to the public next month. You can come back then."

Next month? Tom might already be at a new school in Wichita by next month, but there was no more bargaining with Salvatore. That was quite clear.

Salvatore doesn't know he's messing with an Edison, thought Tom as he stopped to retie his shoe and plucked a crinkled gum wrapper from his pocket. As he ran to catch up with the group, he slipped the wrapper over the door's latch.

"Good luck with your report, young man." Salvatore mussed up Noodle's hair like a friendly uncle before heading toward the escalators.

"So what now?" Colby asked. "Wait till next month?"

"We're going back in," said Tom, spinning on his heel once the curator was safely out of sight.

11
Escape Hatch

Y ou're certifiably insane, you know that? This is just like the time you got me in trouble for helping you calculate the combustion ratios for that hot air balloon." Colby was not pleased about sneaking back into the exhibit. Especially when she was 110 percent positive they were going to get caught.

"That balloon would've worked if we'd bought more propane," said Tom while he inspected *The Alchemy Treatise*'s display case, trying to figure out the best way in.

"It didn't work because you lost interest. Like you do with everything."

Colby had a point. Where Tom's dad was thoughtful and cautious, he was slapdash and distracted. He loved the joy of discovering something new. So much so, he usually couldn't find the patience to see any of his projects to the end.

"Chill out, Colb." Tom had his Swiss Army knife out and was unscrewing the bolts of the display case. "It's not like I'm gonna steal the thing. Just doing some investigation is all."

"As the smooth operator of the group," said Noodle, "I'm gonna have to agree with Colby. I really don't wanna end up in upstate juvie like my third cousin Marty."

"Just stand guard and make sure no one's coming." But no sooner had Tom nudged the glass off the case than a shrill alarm began to sound and swirling red lights were triggered.

"What was that?" Colby squeaked.

"I think I set off one of the sensors!"

"Then why are we still standing here?" yelled Noodle, who was already moving toward the exit.

"Noodle, no!" Panic had crept into Tom's voice. If they got caught, the search would be over like that. "It'll be crawling with guards out there." He quickly replaced the display case and scanned the room for another exit. "We'll have to go through the air-conditioning vents."

"No way. Uh-uh," said Colby, already backing away.

"That's not even close to a normal exit strategy. Once we're in the vent, how would we even get out?"

"I'm sure the ducts lead to, like, a central room or something," Tom assured them. But his friends didn't look too convinced. "Guys, I can't afford to get busted again. My parents'll crucify me."

"This isn't school, bro!" Genuine fear held Noodle's face. "We could get in serious trouble. Like police trouble."

"I promise I can get us out, but you've gotta trust me." There was no more time to waste. Security would be here any second. Tom had his knife out, and within seconds had pried off the vent cover.

"I cannot believe we're actually doing this," Noodle muttered, even as he squeezed into the opening in the wall after Tom. Colby was not far behind.

12
Deeper into the Labyrinth

The siren had grown fainter, and within moments the threesome was enveloped in total darkness. The only sounds they could hear were the clumsy clunking of their elbows and knees against the aluminum vent.

"Betcha anything Salvatore'll just think we set off the alarm on our way out," Tom said into the darkness. He was hoping to calm his friends' nerves as well as his own.

"Let's hope," said Colby. "Otherwise, they'll have to send a search party to find our starved and dehydrated skeletons in the walls." She shivered. "Did I mention I hate it in here?"

"I'm pretty sure he'll figure out what happened when

he sees the vent grate lying on the floor," said Noodle.

"Did you guys hear that?" Colby stopped cold at the sudden hissing and clanking sounds echoing in the distance. "Sounds like a giant snake's up there waiting for us."

"Sounds more like an old furnace to me," said Tom, trying to sound calm even though his stomach was sick with nerves. He'd never done anything remotely this bad before. None of them had.

Up ahead, a tiny pinprick of light lengthened as they inched closer.

"It looks like another vent. Probably where that noise is coming from," said Tom, just as he reached the latticed grate opening that was screwed into the aluminum chute's side. Through the slats, he peered into what looked like a cramped boiler room. One dim lightbulb cast jagged, asymmetrical shadows over a row of humming water tanks and furnaces.

At the far end of the room, he could just make out a skinny iron ladder, bolted to the wall and leading up toward the high ceiling.

"And there's our way out of here." Tom kicked out the

grille and jumped about ten feet to the ground. Colby landed behind him, graceful as a gazelle, while Noodle's long limbs hit the cement at awkward, jutting angles.

"I don't wanna spend one more second in this place than I have to." Colby pushed past Tom and swung her body up onto the shaky ladder with a gymnast's ease. Tom and Noodle followed several paces behind her.

A few rungs up, Tom felt the first wave of fresh terror wash over him. He tried to keep both eyes focused on Colby's sneakers, but his fear of heights was slowing him, and he knew the second he looked down, he would get all dizzy and nervous and probably fall.

"You all right, Tom?" Colby called down to him as if she'd been reading his mind.

"Like you said, the sooner this is over, the better."

"Whenever I'm nervous, I like to do calculations. So, like, if we've been climbing for four minutes, at two rungs per second, each rung equals roughly ten inches. So every minute, if we travel one hundred feet, then—"

"Sweet game, dorkus malorkus," Noodle chimed in from below them. "It's not helping."

Scared as he was, Tom was glad he could at least count on the distraction of his friends.

"Oh my God, oh my God!" yelled Noodle, just as the plinking sound of crashing metal filled the room.

Tom looked down, heart in his throat, to see that his friend was just barely hanging on to the ladder's iron sides. His upturned face was pure fright.

"What happened?"

"The rungs! One of them just gave way under my feet!"

"Are you okay?"

Noodle nodded, gulping down his fear.

"I really think we've made things a lot more complicated than they need to be," he added in a quivering voice, "and I'm kinda starting to regret it."

Tom could feel himself start to lose his cool. Cold sweat prickled on his scalp and at the back of his neck.

Colby was getting way too far up on the ladder.

Noodle was clinging for dear life below.

"It's all right. Everything's going to be okay," he whispered to himself as he clutched his warm hands around one of the rusty metal rungs. But he was pretty sure he wouldn't be able to keep going. His fear of heights had paralyzed him.

"Tom?" He could hear Noodle's voice near his feet.

"You're doing fine. Just put one hand in front of the other. I'm scared to death, too, but if we keep—"

"*Aaaaaaaaahhhhhhhhhh!*"

Above, Colby screamed, a sound as jarring as shattering glass.

13
Emergency Raisins

H ang on, Colb!" Tom called up to her. Climbing unsteadily toward the sound of her screams, he forced his mind to find a calm image—a smoothly operating Nanny Golightly, expertly flipping blueberry pancakes. It wasn't really helping much, but thankfully his instincts had taken over, forcing his hands to keep climbing even as his mind kept telling him to turn around.

At the top of the ladder, he felt relieved to see that Colby had jumped safely onto the upper landing.

"Twenty more rungs and you're done, Noodle," Tom yelled down once he himself was on solid ground. "There's a ledge up here that's wide enough for us all to fit."

"Yup." Noodle's voice was shaky. Tom listened closely to the sounds of his friend cautiously scaling his way to the top and prayed that no more rungs would decide to give way.

Meanwhile, a very terrified Colby couldn't seem to take her eyes off the dark pocket of space above their heads. "Just when I thought it couldn't get worse than a snake." She gulped cartoonishly loud.

"Colby, there's no way a snake could—"

"Just look."

Tom followed her gaze.

He saw the eyes first. Red and poisonous. On the drainpipe above, a huge rat hissed in fury. It was the only thing standing between them and the metal door at the far side of the landing.

"It's okay." Tom could hear the tremor in his own voice. "She's probably more scared of us than we are of her."

"Oh, yeah? She told you that?" Colby's entire body was shaking. "'Cause I didn't hear her say that."

Tom put a finger to his lips as Noodle joined them on the ledge, then took a step closer. The rat bared its yellow fangs.

"Oh, man." Noodle looked ill. "If you'd told me this is was what was waiting for me up here, I might not have kept climbing."

"Got any food on you?" Tom whispered to them.

"Just my emergency raisins." Colby scrounged around in her pockets. "They're a good natural source of sucrose, in case I have an insulin attack."

"Colb, I've known you since you were five." Noodle rolled his eyes. "And I've never heard anything about you having diabetes."

"Well, no. Not technically. But it runs in my family."

Tom bit back a sarcastic retort. Now wasn't the best moment to tease Colby about her phony diseases. There'd be plenty of time for that once they got out of here. If they got out of here.

She handed him a gummy ball of four stuck-together raisins, which Tom rolled into the gum he'd been chewing.

"Hungry there, Mrs. Rat?" He waved the raisin-gum ball in front of the monstrous rodent, enticing her. She raised up on her hind legs, her bald pink nose sniffing, her whiskers twitching.

Tom shivered. It was kind of creepy to have a rat's total attention. He lobbed the food to the far side of the landing, away from them. Annoyed, the rat looked at him, then hopped down from the drainpipe to waddle after it, her tail slithering behind her.

"That should keep her occupied for a bit."

Sure enough, within seconds of tasting the raisin-gum concoction, the rat began chewing noisily, like a dog eating peanut butter.

"Okay, let's go," said Tom. "That door has got to lead us to somewhere better than here."

And it probably did. But unfortunately, it was locked.

"All that climbing up," complained Noodle, "and now there aren't even enough rungs on that ladder for us to get back down."

"But there is another one of these." Tom tapped the air vent next to the door, and started to unscrew its grate. "It's our only option." But the screws were rusty and painted over. He had to push hard to get them to budge.

"And it looks like word's hit the streets about the food." Noodle nodded toward another rodent that had materialized on the drainpipe and was peering down at them. The rat leaped, brushing against Noodle's white sneakers.

"Watch it! Don't scuff the new kicks!" He kicked at a third, even fatter rat that had scuttled out from under a hole in the wall. It let out a piercing shriek and showed its ugly teeth.

"These rats could be walked on a leash." Colby's body

was plastered against the wall. "Tom, hurry up with that vent."

"Gross. They're everywhere!" Noodle was hopping and kicking now as he tried to keep the rodents away from him.

The air was vibrant, echoing with the vicious squeaking. There were nearly a dozen rats on the landing now, nibbling at the gum and raisins.

"Got it!" Tom finally pulled the grate off the vent, and the three of them scrambled inside the wide crawl space as fast as they could.

Finally, the rats were gone, and after a few minutes of crawling, the group approached yet another set of vent slats. But as soon as Tom peered through the opening, he realized they had a whole other problem.

14
Free as a...

What is this place?"

The bird's-eye view showed a bright, airy atrium with a dark tiled floor, potted plants, and an ornate fountain in the middle of the room.

Noodle craned his neck. "We're still in the Met, I think. I see a sign that says no eating or drinking or cell phones. Definite museum-y rules."

"Must be one of the wings." Tom recalled seeing tons of side rooms and offshoot exhibits on the museum's webpage last night.

"Think those trees are real? 'Cause if they could support me, I bet I could make the jump from that big shade thing over there." Colby was nodding toward an enormous piece of fabric hanging down from a nearby archway.

"That's a terrible idea."

"Yeah, don't mess with the order of our crew," said Noodle. "*Tom's* the daredevil who does the stupid stuff to get himself killed. You're just the brains, remember?"

"It's a simple level-one dismount." She was breathing deeply to steady her nerves. "Only without a net to catch me."

"Look," said Tom, "I'm the one who got us into this mess. So I should be the one to get us out."

But Colby shook her head no. She had her grip ready, and there was no dissuading her. "Just open the grate before I chicken out."

Tom used one of his pocketknife's wrench attachments to twist off the vent's long screws. The guys watched in amazement as Colby took one final calming breath and kicked out her legs through the grate. She looked so frail swinging out against the atrium backdrop, then arcing gracefully toward the hanging fabric. Her fingers grabbed its bottom, and her body swung in like a trapeze artist.

"Colby? Colby!"

"I don't think I'm gonna make it," she called back, now hanging there forty feet above the ground.

Museum patrons came running as soon as they heard the commotion.

"There's a girl up there!"

"Where did she come from?"

"She just fell out of the sky!"

"That's impossible!"

"I'm cool," Colby called down to the small crowd. "I can pretty much hang up here forever."

But more people had gathered below, their stares and shouts echoing throughout the courtyard. Cell phones were pulled out—a few to call for help, but others to snap photos of the girl dangling in the middle of the archway.

Within seconds, a troop of uniformed guards came running, with walkie-talkies unsheathed as they radioed for back up.

"Yep, that's it," said Tom. "We're toast."

15
Roundup

"On a college application, does 'convicted felon' go under extracurriculars or sports?" Noodle cracked his knuckles and fidgeted restlessly.

The threesome were seated in a line of folding chairs inside Lieutenant Ellen Faber's nondescript office at the Central Park Precinct police station. Through the double-glazed window, Tom could see his mom and dad, along with Colby's nana and Noodle's mom, standing outside, talking with the grim-faced police officer.

His mother's expression was especially tense.

This is bad, Tom thought. Even though Faber had agreed to let them off with only a warning, he figured that being in trouble with his parents would still be way worse than anything the police could legally do to him.

"I bet you Faber only said we could leave so that we'd let our guard down," Colby whispered. "Ever hear of good cop, bad cop? She'll be bringing in the bad cop any second, trust me."

"You're probably right," said Noodle.

Just then, Lieutenant Faber entered the room, followed by Tom's parents, Noodle's mom, and Colby's nana.

"Oh, my little Bernard!" Mrs. Zuckerberg cried, hugging Noodle and then giving him a twist on the ear the way she always did when he did something that both scared and upset her. Mrs. Z tended to be all of the overs: overprotective, overemotional, and generally overinvolved. "The thought of my baby at the police station. Dragged in like some criminal."

"Ma!" protested a beet-faced Noodle. "You watch too much *CSI*."

Lieutenant Faber cleared her throat, bringing the room to silence, before she took a seat behind her desk, folded her hands primly, and jumped into her lecture. "I'm sure you three are fully aware of how worried and upset we all are. Breaking into a closed exhibit—"

"But we didn't steal anything," Tom interrupted.

Faber shot him an icy stare, almost baiting him to keep talking.

"Sorry." Tom placed a hand over his mouth and slouched low in his chair.

"Breaking into a closed exhibit, then having to be rescued from the air-conditioning vents by the fire department."

From the corner of his eye, Tom looked over at his mother, who was sitting in her chair, tight-lipped and poker-faced, which made her seem all the more scary.

"Fortunately," continued Faber, "the museum has agreed not to press charges. In so doing, however—"

"Here it comes," Noodle muttered, with another loud crack of the knuckles. "So long, NYU drama scholarship. Hello, lockdown."

Faber's lips pressed together. It was clear she'd had about enough of these kids interrupting her day.

"In so doing, however, you are all on one-year probation from entering the Met." Her pale green eyes studied Tom for a long moment, and he couldn't help feeling like there was something else behind her gaze. Something mistrustful.

"I assure you, ma'am." Now Tom's dad spoke up,

adjusting his glasses nervously, then wiping his palms on his grease-stained khakis. "These are good kids. This will never happen again."

"Let's hope so." Faber stood up from her chair and swept around the group to open her office door. "I hope to never see you all in here again. You kids could've seriously hurt yourselves."

As he exited the office, Faber gave Tom's dad a steady once-over. "So you're really Thomas Edison's great-grandson?"

"I am." He puffed up a little. Tom wished he'd worn a less wrinkly shirt and that the fingerprint wasn't so visible on his glasses lens.

Faber nodded, not too impressed by what she saw.

The kids shuffled out the door with their heads held low like badly behaved puppies. "Hanging there in the middle of the courtyard!" Tom heard Colby's grandmother hiss. "I almost fainted when they told me. And I'm sure those vents are completely toxic, teeming with strange dust mites and allergens. You'll catch an infection and be in an iron lung, sure as I'm standing here."

"I feel fine, Nana," said Colby, "and I don't think they even make iron lungs anymore."

Tom walked past the maze

station's entrance, when he happe

Faber standing near the back hallw

She was talking to a portly man in a bla

tight at every place on his body. The man

an exploding tube of cookie dough that

sweaty bald head.

The man glanced up and held Tom's gaze with

so unnerving that Tom could feel himself getting fu

The man's eyes narrowed into slits, and it felt like he wa

searing Tom's identity into his brain, filing it away for

future use.

Faber placed a hand on the fat man's shoulder and led

him into her office, but before closing the door, she also

locked eyes with Tom for a split second. It felt like they

were issuing him some kind of warning. About what,

though, he had no idea.

Spooked, he turned on his heel and sprinted, bursting

through the precinct doors and out onto the sidewalk—

and wasn't sure what to make of what he saw next.

His parents stood together on the bottom step, speak-

ing in low tones. As Tom neared, he saw his mom twist

off her wedding band and, with a nod, place it in his dad's

Now Tom was close enough to make out their over-
ing waves of conversation.

"No, no," his dad said. "What kind of—"

"Just talk to Pete," his mother interrupted. "He'll help."
She leaned in and kissed his father's cheek.

"You're the light of my life, do you know that?" said
his father, with a smile so warm and soupy it could have
fogged over his glasses.

"Hi, Mom. Hi, Dad." Tom approached with caution,
testing the parental waters.

"Well, if it isn't the man of the hour." His dad shook
his head. "I'm still not sure what this latest stunt merits in
terms of punishment."

"And we haven't even addressed your little science-
class escapade yet either," added his mom flatly.

"What were you all even doing in that exhibit?"

They were coming at him from all angles. Tom wondered if he was ever going to see the light of day again.

"Mom, Dad. You know I'm sorry to the millionth
degree. And I would just like to point out that, although
it was my first brush with the law, it involved a very
respected museum, no damages, and no technical violation of—"

His mother had her hand up, crossing-guard style. "Thomas Alva Edison, why do you always have to see how far the rules bend before they break?"

"I know I messed up, but I'll do all the dishes, all the housework," said Tom. "Just please, please, please don't ground me. Not on my last spring break in New York, with my best friends, who I'll never get to see once we move. I haven't even had a chance to break the news to them yet. I can't even think about telling them, and then not even getting to see them."

He had been rehearsing this impassioned speech in his head, hoping it would hit all the right emotional marks without overdoing it. Tough to tell. His mom and dad both looked exhausted, like they already had a zillion things on their minds.

"We'll discuss this tonight," said his mom. "I have to get back to my sister's and pick up Rose, and your father needs to run an errand in town." But Tom could tell by her softening tone that his speech just might have struck a nerve. Given the circumstances of their move, maybe there would be no grounding after all.

"I'm just so disappointed in you," she added before heading to her car.

"I'm sorry, Mom," said Tom. He truly meant it, too. Ever since setting off his first combustion explosion in third grade, he knew he'd caused his parents enough stress and worry to last five lifetimes.

For some reason, he just couldn't ever seem to see the consequences of his actions, no matter how extreme or dangerous.

And now thanks to all his thoughtlessness, Tom was never going to get his hands on *The Alchemy Treatise*. That much, he knew.

16
Dropping the Bomb

"My ma's gotta head back to work, too," said Noodle as he approached Tom and his dad on their way to the car. "Is it cool if you guys give me a lift home, Mr. E?"

"Sure, Noodle," answered Tom's dad. "But I've got a quick detour to make."

"Thanks. Shotgun!" He already had his hand on the door to the Edison family station wagon and was lounging comfortably in the front seat before Tom had a chance to protest.

With the caution of an old lady at a busy intersection, Mr. Edison pulled onto Central Park West and headed uptown. He was out of his element driving in Manhattan and puttered along at seven miles an hour, hugging the right-hand line, while yellow taxis honked and swerved past him on all sides. It took them well over an hour and a half just to get out of the city.

Southeast Yonkers, where the Edison family called home, was like a lot of towns in the outer boroughs. Brick, bland, and boring, with mom-and-pop hardware stores, pharmacies, and an Italian restaurant on practically every corner. As soon as they merged onto Midland Avenue, Tom's dad began what Tom thought of as the "vulture circle"—wheeling around and around the same blocks, in hope of finding that elusive parking spot.

Noodle had commandeered the radio and didn't even notice when Tom's dad missed two free spaces.

"Dad!" Tom pressed forward, pointing. "There! And there . . . and there."

"Oh, right—thanks." Mr. Edison craned his neck to reverse the station wagon at a snail's pace into a massive spot by the curb. As he put the car in park, Tom caught his dad's eyes in the rearview mirror. They looked troubled and distant. "Why don't you two go hang out at Sammy's for a bit? And I'll meet you back here in twenty minutes."

"Sure," said Tom. "Where are you going, anyway?"

"Just a couple things I need to take care of."

Something was definitely up. Even Noodle raised his eyebrows. "Mr. Mystery," he murmured as the three of them stepped out of the car.

At their first stop, Sammy's Electronics, the wire adapters Tom had been waiting for still hadn't come in, so they decided to kill time at their mutually favorite haunt, Lucky Lou's Five and Dime, one of the several run-down retail shops along Midland.

Inside the stuffy, overstocked store, Noodle swept a rainbow wig off one of the shelves, fixing it onto his head as he checked his reflection in a tiny mirror by the front counter. Lucky Lou himself was in his normal spot, snoozing away behind the front register while an *I Love Lucy* rerun played on his tiny black-and-white TV.

"Noodle, I have something I really need to get off my chest." Tom had planted himself directly in his friend's path. "It's been killing me."

"Literally? You're not dying, are you?"

"No. Worse. My dad just took some job in Wichita." Tom let the words hang in the stale air for a moment. Noodle's mouth opened slightly, and his eyes drifted to the side, like he was trying to figure out a strange riddle in his head.

"What do you mean, Wichita?" he finally said.

"Like, halfway across the country. Kansas. We're moving in two weeks."

"When were you gonna tell me?"

"I just found out two days ago."

"Is this for . . . forever?"

Tom shrugged. "For a while. Probably till I'm in college."

"You can't do that," said Noodle dryly. "We have too much stuff to do. There's like, puberty and driving and, and, and . . ." His gaze was bouncing around the room, and his voice was growing louder. "We were supposed to get part-time jobs together at Pie in the Sky, remember? Now who am I gonna learn to toss pizza dough with? You know everyone else at school annoys me!"

"At least you have Colby. I'm losing my two best friends, and I'm not gonna know anyone."

"Your dad's whole plan is Craisins! You're from New York." Noodle was pleading with Tom now, as if he'd been the one who'd decided to move. "People in the

Midwest'll think you're like some kind of a Martian with your weird inventions and stuff."

"Richard Drew invented Scotch tape, and he was from Minnesota."

"You're missing the point. Which is that this is the worst news ever."

Tom had been dreading this conversation for a while, and though he was thankful for it to be over, it had gone as terribly as he thought it would, and he didn't feel the least bit better now that the secret was off his chest. In fact, on top of all the dread, he now felt guilty for letting down his friend.

Too depressed to continue their conversation, Noodle gave the turnstile of sunglasses a hard, squeaky spin, then wandered off toward the souvenir section, where Lou kept the shelves stocked with New York shot glasses and postcards.

Alone in the aisle, Tom distracted himself by absent-mindedly inspecting the inside of a cheap FM radio in search of a frequency scanner for Nanny Golightly. Since there was no foreseeable way to continue the treasure hunt, which probably never existed in the first place, he would have to turn all his attention and hope back to her. Even though she was shaping up to be another bust like all the others.

As he neared the front of the store, he saw his father through the windows of Kreger & Sons Pawnshop across the street. Tom couldn't make out much, but it looked like his dad was in a deep conversation with Pete Kreger, the shop's owner.

Talk to Pete, his mom had said.

"I'll meet you back at the car," Tom yelled to Noodle as he walked out of Lucky Lou's.

"Wait! Tom," he heard Noodle call back, "you need to see this."

But Tom was too distracted. He ducked out of sight, then scrambled across the street toward Kreger's.

17
Bands of Hope

Peering through the front window, Tom saw that Pete was inspecting an item of jewelry through his magnifying glass. It was a green emerald ring. And sitting next to it on the counter was the Firestone negative, which had now been enlarged to a photo!

Tom pushed through the front doors.

"Dad! What's going on?"

"Thought I said to meet me at the car." Tom saw a flash of gold as his dad quickly shoved something small and metal into his pocket.

"When did you have the photo enlarged? And why are you selling it?"

"This morning, and I'm not selling it. I'm just ...

getting it appraised." His dad looked to Pete, who nodded slightly.

"'Fraid the best I could do is seventy-five," said Pete. "Even if it's authentic."

"And what about that ring?" Tom asked. His dad was silent for a moment, shifting his weight uncomfortably.

"Just scraping together a little extra cash for the move." He looked especially uneasy when Pete pulled the ring off the black velvet cloth and handed it over.

Tom quickly snatched it from Pete's fingers, and his heart began pounding through his chest as he looked closer. Running along the side of the emerald, formed in gold, he saw the entwined rose, the circle . . . it was the same symbol that had been stamped beneath the riddle. And the painting of Theodore Roosevelt.

Tom's suspicions were right. His father had to know more than he was letting on.

"It's a family piece. Your grandpa gave it to me when I was a kid," Mr. Edison explained.

"What is it?"

"He called it his ring of the Sub Rosa."

"What's the Sub Rosa?" Tom asked. "And how come you've never told me about it?"

His dad ran a hand through his shaggy salt-and-pepper hair, and Tom could see something was making him nervous.

"It was nothing. Just some secret club of artists and scientists and people like that."

"From when?"

"I don't know. It started sometime in the late eighteen hundreds, I think. Lasted for about fifty years."

One thing Tom knew about his dad: the man was incapable of lying. Even if he was reluctant to divulge the information, Tom was certain he'd eventually get what he needed out of him.

"Was Thomas Edison in the Sub Rosa?"

"Uh-huh." His dad nodded, relaxing a tiny bit. "And according to your grandpa, who was not the most credible source, mind you, so were all sorts of people along the way: FDR, Henry Ford, even Babe Ruth, at one point."

"Teddy Roosevelt and Harvey Firestone were part of it, too, I bet."

Pete gave Tom's dad a wink. "You're just tryin' to jack the price up on me."

"What was the purpose of the club? Why'd they keep it so secret?" The questions were coming faster than Tom could process them.

His dad let out a heavy sigh as he knelt down to pluck the ring out of Tom's palm. The emerald seemed to wink as he held it up to the afternoon sunlight.

"Well, as the legend goes," his father continued, "this ring is a symbol of the Sub Rosa's promise to guard the most—" He stopped midsentence, as if he wanted to say more but thought better of it.

"What? The promise to guard the most what?" Tom asked.

"No. Forget it. I don't want to go filling your head with Grandpa's wild dreams. Especially after what you put us through this morning." His dad's fingers enveloped the ring as he stood up and handed it back to Mr. Kreger. "How much, Pete?"

"Dad, please don't sell it!" Tom practically shouted.

"Your grandfather's imagination is exactly what got him into trouble. Kind of like someone else I know."

"Sorry to burst your bubble, Mr. Edison, but the emerald's fake." Pete shrugged his shoulders matter-of-factly.

"See? It's not even worth anything," said Tom. "All the more reason to keep it." Relief washed over him. "The ring belongs to us, it's our history. Please. I'm begging you."

His dad wavered for a moment before finally relenting.

"Fine, the ring can stay in the family. Though I don't think you're in a position to be bargaining with anybody."

"Thank you so much, Dad."

"Now get going. I'll be out in a minute."

As Tom exited Pete's store, he bent low out of view, then peered back through the front door to see the golden glimmer of his parents' wedding bands reappear from his father's pocket. He watched in shock as Pete examined the rings through the jeweler's lens. Tom's stomach was now sinking into his knees. Until that moment, he'd had no idea his parents' financial situation was so dire.

Walking back to the car, he was so lost in thought and worry that he nearly collided straight into a breathless Noodle.

"Dude! I was trying to find you everywhere. Check this out."

He pulled a black-and-white postcard out of a small Lucky Lou's paper bag. "Ebbets Field. Where the Brooklyn Dodgers used to play."

Tom gave it a quick glance. "Cool."

"You're not seeing it." Noodle placed his hand over one side of the postcard, so that only the edge of the stadium's outfield wall was visible. "Now does it ring a bell?"

Tom gave it a second, longer look.

"No way." He snatched the postcard out of Noodle's hands. "No freaking way!"

But it was unmistakable. The curved, brick edge of the stadium perfectly matched the window's view in the photograph of Harvey Firestone.

It wasn't much, but it was something.

ColBeans: I can't believe u told Noodle b4 me!! >:O

TE iv: didn't wanna freak every1 out

RamenNoodle: focus, u 2. r we still on 4 2day???
   C's casa??

ColBeans: 1st gotta help N w/chores ☹. bye!

All things considered, their punishments had been tough but manageable. Six p.m. curfew for the rest of spring break. No allowance indefinitely. And the three of them could only spend time at one another's houses under parental supervision. As upset as Tom's parents had been, the family move date had also been set for the end of the month, so they understood his need to spend every second he could with Colby and Noodle.

What they didn't know was the search to find the secret of the Sub Rosa was back on, and it had a new headquarters: Colby's backyard tent.

That way, as she had explained on IM, her nana couldn't barge in unannounced.

Besides, Noodle's house was way too tough a location, thanks to Mrs. Zuckerberg's constant, parole officer–like monitoring of her son's every move.

And at Tom's house, the packing tape and brown storage boxes were already starting to appear, and if there was a worse sight than that, he couldn't think of it.

"You're going to have to make a few choices about what comes with us and what stays behind." Tom's mother swung into his room as he quickly minimized his IM screen. "And you know what I'm talking about." She meant his basement lab, of course—since a lot of his stuff might be termed "junk" by the less enlightened. Just the thought of starting a new lab in Wichita gave him the sweats.

After cleaning up the family's lunch dishes as part of his punishment, Tom set off into the clean spring air. He'd been making this walk to Colby's, down Heath Street with a left onto Poplar, since he was seven years old.

The idea that in a couple of weeks he'd never pass this way again was crushing. He knew every pothole and broken sidewalk stone as well as he knew his own face.

Inside the tent they'd pitched in Colby's backyard, Tom found Noodle sitting cross-legged, pecking away on his laptop, with a mountain of snacks, candy, chips, and soda cans splayed all around him.

"I raided the pantry before I left," he said as Tom zipped open the flap.

"Awesome."

Tom didn't waste a second tearing into a packet of chocolate chip cookies like a hungry bear. His mom kept the cupboard stocked with dried fruit leathers and organic wheat cereal that tasted like tree bark, so it was always fun to gorge himself whenever he got to sleep over at chez Zuckerberg.

Tom was waiting for it, but Noodle had decided to avoid the subject of Wichita and concentrate instead on his laptop. Still, Tom saw that there were dark circles under his friend's eyes, and he had a feeling Noodle's sleep had been as bad as his.

To temporarily distract himself from family moves and unsolvable treasure hunts, Tom had spent part of the night sketching a prototype for his new spoon-shaped Q-tip—infinitely more effective for scooping out earwax than the regular kind, and an invention that might, if all else failed, put his family back on the map.

"Find anything on the Sub Rosa or alchemy?" said Tom as he crumpled up and pitched the cookie wrapper before diving into some Doritos.

"No, but I did lay the vocals from *High School Musical Three* over the instrumentals off Lil Wayne's new album. I'm calling it *Reform School Remixed.*"

"Really helpful, Noodle." Tom opened his backpack and pulled out all his research on *The Alchemy Treatise* and Teddy Roosevelt, plus the sun-and-moon riddle from the camera, a Xerox copy of the Firestone photo that he'd managed to make last night, and the Ebbets Field postcard. It was everything they had, so far.

"I only went on GarageBand because I couldn't find squat online about the Sub Rosa," said Noodle. "It's either the most secret club in history, or it never existed in the first place."

"Which is all the more reason this treasure hunt has to be real. Why go through all the trouble unless secrecy was absolutely necessary?"

"So what? You think Edison, like, invented a way to make gold or something?" said Noodle.

"Sure would make all our lives easier."

Of course, the thought had occurred to all of them in private, but it just seemed too preposterous to believe. Still, the hope of a golden formula or some kind of secret treasure kept nagging at the back of Tom's mind like an invisible mosquito, whispering to him every so often and forcing him to keep digging for answers.

"Sorry I'm late. Nana made me put on SPF-fifty for the five-second walk out here." Colby's face appeared between the flaps. She was holding a binder of papers in her hands. "I did make a tiny breakthrough, though. It's not a lot, but . . . I found a blueprint of Ebbets Field online, then did an advanced key-phrase cross-reference in the city archives. Words like *gold, sun, moon, Sub Rosa, Edison*—"

"Colb, your dork meter's off the charts right now," Noodle interrupted. "Slooooowww it down."

"Here, see for yourself." She shoved a piece of paper into his hands and caught her breath. "Second paragraph."

Noodle read. "'Overlooking the Ebbets Field bleachers is the Robinson Sundial, named for longtime Dodgers' manager Wilbert Robinson.'"

Tom and Noodle went silent.

"I don't get the connection," Tom said after a moment. "Unless this Robinson guy was friends with Henry Ford or something."

"Or he was in the Sub Rosa."

"'One hundred yards north of the sun and moon.' Like it says in the riddle." Colby looked from Tom to Noodle as though she were dealing with preschoolers. "Sun and moon? Sundials? Ebbets Field's in the photo? It has a famous sundial. Do I have to spell it out for you?"

"That's a bit of a stretch," said Tom.

"And Ebbets Field was torn down, like, fifty years ago."

"Okay, sure, but if the room where this photo was taken still exists," said Colby, "it might lead us somewhere."

"Maybe." Noodle's fingers were already flying over the keys. "I can find the stadium's old address."

Tom glanced at his watch. "If we left now, two hours to get to Brooklyn, look for clues, plus two hours back. We might be able to make it home by curfew."

"Nana'll be asleep until dinner," said Colby, "but we'll have to go through the McFaddens' yard just to be safe."

"Who knows? Maybe we'll find something." Tom

shrugged, throwing all the papers into his bag and stepping out into the sunlight. "And it's not like we're doing anything dangerous or illegal. It's just research."

"Like an extra-credit project," Colby added.

It was settled then. Next stop, Brooklyn . . .

19
Clued In

"I don't see any sundials." Colby yawned.

"And I'm seriously losing steam." Noodle flopped down onto a patch of grass next to the sidewalk. The three of them had been searching this run-down neighborhood of Flatbush in Brooklyn for an hour and a half. So far, nothing.

"Yeah, this is pointless. That photo could have been taken from anywhere in this entire neighborhood." Colby collapsed onto the curb next to Noodle.

Tom stepped back, scanning the south side of Sullivan Place, a street that was little more than a crumbling block of row houses, a few shabby storefronts, and a scaffolded parking garage.

On the other side of them was a cluster of high-rise

apartments where, half a century ago, Ebbets Field had once stood like a towering castle.

"Okay, if the entrance to the ballpark was over there . . ." Tom stared at the apartment buildings, trying to picture the baseball stadium. It was impossible to mentally position where the photo would have been taken. There were simply too many variables.

What is the missing piece? he wondered to himself for the hundredth time that afternoon.

"Betcha Big T's in heaven looking down on us right now, laughing at what idiots we are." Noodle stared up at the cloudless sky. *"I invent ze lightbulb, and zey can't even zolve a few clues? Vat is ze matter vit zese bratvurtzes?"*

"That's a really good imitation of Albert Einstein, dummy." Colby smirked. "But I don't think Thomas Edison had a German accent, considering he was from Ohio." She plucked a few strands of grass and mindlessly drizzled them over the sidewalk curb. "Let's get outta here," she called over to Tom. "My nana'll be up from her nap soon."

"We can't go!" he called back. "We're already at the Bed, Ford!"

"I get that's a reference to the camera riddle." Noodle stretched his arms over his head. "But I have zero idea what you're blabbing about."

"He capitalized the *B* in *Bed*!" Tom was hopping up and down, motioning them over. "It wasn't referring to Henry Ford at all."

"Still not following." Colby shook her head as Noodle and she stood up and jogged over toward Tom, who was smiling wide and staring up at the street sign marking the intersection of Sullivan Place and Bedford Avenue.

Tom pulled the scrap of paper from where he kept it folded in his wallet, and reread the riddle. "'When you reach the Bed, Ford. You're just one hundred yards north of the sun and moon.'"

"So this whole time," Noodle wondered aloud, "all we had to do was start at Bedford and go a hundred yards south?"

"Three feet equals one yard," blurted Colby.

"You just can't resist, can you?" Noodle smirked.

Tom was already counting out his paces down the street. The others quickly fell into step.

Ninety-eight . . . ninety-nine . . . one hundred.

At the hundredth yard, they looked up.

On one side, the road. On the other side, a dilapidated townhouse's peeling facade and dark windows dared them to enter.

"This place so does not look up to code," said Colby. "Also, as a side note, I'm getting a slightly haunted vibe."

"Maybe...but check that out." The others followed Noodle's gaze, now fixed above the house's slated roof, to the wrought-iron weather vane above the chimney.

A large gray stone sun and moon were fastened to its crest.

"Wherever we are, we're here," said Tom as they climbed the narrow front steps to the building's screened door, which opened with a push and creak...

...leading them straight to a dingy vestibule.

"Noodle, your cell phone is in range, right?" Colby crossed her arms in front of her chest. "This place looks like kidnapper central."

"Nothing that exciting. It's a pet shop," said Noodle, pointing to the purple block-lettered sign that read,

MITZI'S PETS

"But before that, it was this." Tom tapped the brass plaque next to the intercom.

Together, they all read the New York landmark engraving.

This building formerly housed The Vesper Inn.
An artist-only boardinghouse,
where F. Scott Fitzgerald, Mary Cassatt,
and Mark Twain once lodged.

"The Vesper Inn," said Noodle. "Why didn't they just say so?"

"Too easy," said Colby. "If you're in the Sub Rosa, why tell it straight when you can turn it into an insane wild goose chase?"

The others weren't sure how to answer that one.

"Well, I'm going in," said Tom.

20
Meeting Mitzi

A bell jangled as they pushed in through the door, setting off a wild orchestra of barks, meows, and chirps.

In cases and cages, burrowed-in or on show-off display, small animals, from furry to spiny to scaly, were everywhere.

But there was not a single human in sight. Tom checked the area. Nobody was behind the cash register or tending to the animals. Faintly, from a back room behind the front counter, came the far-off hum of a vacuum cleaner.

Colby sneezed. "Sorry. Too much fur and feathers for my sinuses."

"Shh." Tom motioned for them to follow him down a windowless hallway that was banked on both sides with blue-lit, glubbing aquariums. "If anyone comes in and asks what we're doing, just say we're looking for a sales-person," he whispered.

"I'm getting Met déjà vu," remarked Colby as they tip-toed down the hallway.

The floorboards creaked under the weight of their shoes.

"This place is so super old," whispered Noodle.

"It even smells old," Colby added. "Don't you think it's kinda weird to convert a house like this into a pet store? It looks nothing like the ones you see at the mall."

"Mall pet shops are depressing," said Noodle. "At night, everyone leaves—"

"What don't you two understand about *shh*?" Tom put a finger to his lips as the corridor opened up into a side room, sandbagged on one end with floor-to-ceiling feed and cedar-chip bags, as well as stacked cages of snakes and lizards.

It was lit only by the indirect sunlight through a large window that faced out onto the street. The view was of the Ebbets Field Apartments, but there was no way to know for sure if this was the same room where Firestone's photo had been taken all those years ago.

Until Noodle glanced up at the ceiling rafters and saw

the intricate painted pattern of family crests and fleurs-de-lis above their heads.

"This is it, you guys!" He pointed toward the ceiling. "This is the spot!"

"Say it a little louder. They might not have heard you back in Yonkers." But as Tom stepped back to get a better look at the rafters, it was clear Noodle was right.

Tom reached into his backpack to grab the notebook where he'd put the Firestone photo and held it up in front of their faces, trying to position the picture in the exact spot where the old man would have been sitting.

From this angle, with the window behind him... "Firestone's definitely pointing toward that far wall," said Tom.

"Totally. His hand's all stiff and posed." In the air, Colby traced the arc of his finger.

Whatever Firestone was trying to show us, Tom thought. *It had to be located behind those cages of—*

"Lizards!" Noodle shouted. "He's pointing behind the lizard cages!"

"Will you stop screaming like that? Someone's gonna—*arghhh*!" Tom jumped, slapping the back of his neck, where something very sharp had bitten him.

Dustbuster in one hand, lettuce-green parrot on her opposite shoulder, an old woman had crept up on them silently. Woman and parrot were now staring at the three kids with similar, unblinking eyes.

"Hey!" Tom rubbed the sore spot. "Your parrot bit me."

"Yoo-Hoo is my security system," the old woman snapped. "Never met a neck he didn't like. I'm Mitzi."

Tom had never seen anyone like Mitzi. She was taller than most men, with multiple gray, frizzy braids hanging down her back, and just as many stacks of clattering plastic bracelets weighting both arms.

Clankingly, she pointed at Tom, Colby, and Noodle in turn. "Australian shepherd, American bobtail cat, and"—her finger hovered over Noodle's head like a divining rod—"praying mantis."

"Is that a riddle we have to solve so you won't, um, broil us?" inquired Colby.

"Those are your animal counterparts," the woman answered. "If this were a magical world, they'd be your familiars. Unfortunately, we're in Brooklyn. You're here to find a pet?"

"What about me screams *praying mantis* to you?" Noodle sounded half offended, half curious.

Tom offered Mitzi what he hoped was his most charming smile. "Maybe we'll get Noodle a praying mantis next time. See, my friend here wants a dog. Really, really bad. And he heard you made the best pet connections in all the boroughs." He slung an arm over Noodle's shoulders, then pivoted him in Mitzi's direction. "Work with me," he whispered in his friend's ear.

"You heard that right." Mitzi arched her brows. "But you won't find a dog in the reptile room. Follow me, Mantis." The woman wafted out into the hallway; Tom prodded Noodle with a helpful push.

"No way, T. You better not be leaving me alone with that—"

"Noodle, you're the smooth operator," Tom hissed back. "Be charming. Make her laugh with your jokes. Pet the puppies. It'll buy us some time to check the place out."

"Maaaaan-tis!" Mitzi trilled from down the hall. "I'm sure we can find you a dog!"

"Maaaaan-tis!" squawked Yoo-Hoo.

"That's your cue," said Colby. "Mantis!"

21
Behind the Cages

Once Mitzi and Noodle had left the room, Tom and Colby wasted no time squeezing themselves between the two towers of stacked glass cages. In one cage, a diamond-backed snake reared back, its tiny fangs bared at Colby. She instinctively moved a little closer to Tom and shuddered. Colby was on overload, trying hard to be nonphobic in the face of all these germy animals.

"On three. Lift and slide." As Tom's fingertips hooked under two corners of a bottom cage, readying himself, three salamanders scurried to its other end and stared up at him with black, unblinking eyes.

"One . . . two . . . three . . ." The metal screeched against the wood.

"She mighta heard that," said Colby, cutting her eyes toward the door.

They waited, breath held, for Mitzi and Yoo-Hoo to come storming into the room, but there was no sign of them. Tom and Colby were in the clear. For now.

Tom turned toward the now exposed brick wall behind the stack of cages. At first glance, it didn't look too promising, so he ran his hand along its rough surface, his fingers searching the braille-like grooves for some sort of clue. And then he felt something.

Near the bottom of the wall, in the middle of the brick, was a small indentation and a smooth patch no bigger than a quarter. He knelt, his face inches from the floor, and came eye to eye with an encircled rose imprint etched into the brick.

"Colb!" he whispered loudly. "Over here. It's the seal of the Sub Rosa!"

"Shut up!" Her jaw was on the floor as she huddled in close next to Tom. "Up till now, this all seemed too far-fetched . . . but . . ." She reached her hand out to touch the sanded grooves of the rose petals.

The mortar surrounding the brick was a different

texture, Tom realized. Lighter, too, as if it had been more recently replaced. Something must be hidden behind that brick.

"How can we get to it?" Tom wondered aloud. "Ugh. I never have C-four explosives when I need them."

"That's one sentence you are never, ever allowed to say in the presence of my nana."

Tom leaned against the wall and wracked his brain. Mitzi would be back soon—even Noodle couldn't keep her occupied forever—and there was no way to get through that brick. In a week and a half, he'd be in Kansas and might never get an opportunity like this again. If he could just get his hands on a strong acid.

Vinegar's acidic, Tom thought. *But not enough, unless I combine it with something corrosive.*

Chemical combinations and reactions swirled through his mind at rapid-fire speed, years and years of basement experiments coming back to him.

After a moment, Tom popped to his feet, snapping his fingers.

"All right, Colb," he said, turning to her, his face the picture of focus. "We need to split up."

"Uh-uh, Tom. I know that look. What's going on inside that brain of yours?"

"I can't explain right now, but chemically speaking, this should work."

"On second thought, I don't even wanna know what—"

"I know you don't. But we don't have time. You need to go to the bathroom, get us some powdered bleach, a plastic bucket if you can find one, and a whole buncha paper towels. And whatever you do, don't let Mitzi see you."

Colby was about to rattle off the top twenty reasons why whatever Tom was thinking about doing was a terrible idea, but something stopped her. Maybe it was the pleading look in his eyes. Maybe it was the excitement about what could be behind that wall. Or maybe Colby McCracken had become so used to the sneaking and risk taking of this odd treasure hunt that she'd grown a teeny bit braver these past few days. Whatever the reason, she found herself nodding her head.

"Okay, I'll do it. What about you?"

Tom hesitated, surprised by her response, then smiled, with eyes glimmering mischievously. "I'm going through that window. We'll meet back in five, so you can hoist me up."

"Cool."

Placing trust in her friend when safe logic and sound reasoning had failed her, Colby disappeared into the hallway.

22
A Chocolate Solution

On their hundred-yard walk to the pet store, Tom remembered seeing Mel's Grocery Mart, a shabby little convenience store on Bedford, but with Mitzi in the front room, probably explaining to Noodle the pros and cons of cockapoos versus schnauzer doodles, there was only one way to get there without arousing too much suspicion.

Paint had gummed the window shut, but after a few heaves, he was finally able to force it open a crack. After that, it was just a three-foot drop to the sidewalk.

Hurrying across the street, he noticed a black Cadillac parked along the curb. Its windows were tinted, and its engine was running. Tom could make out a shadowed figure in dark glasses slumped behind the wheel, but he was too nervous to take a longer look at the driver's face. Instead he stared straight down at his shoelaces until he was safely inside Mel's.

The convenience store was bare-bones and dusty, and most of the items on the shelves looked to be way past their expiration dates. Tom was still able to assemble all the ingredients he needed: vinegar, salt, baking soda, dish-washing gloves, a plastic jug of springwater, and a Hershey's bar. Weighted down, he approached the register, pulling a twenty-dollar bill from his wallet. Good-bye to a month's savings.

"An investment," Tom mumbled to comfort himself as a shaggy, incurious teen rang him up.

He grabbed his change, a measly $1.17, and slipped back out the jingling door. Outside, the Cadillac had been vacated. Tom stopped to peek through the window. What a mess. The backseat was littered with fast-food wrappers and empty soda cups, plus sun-faded magazines and newspapers. Whoever drove that car spent a lot of time in it.

"You're just being paranoid over nothing," Tom said to himself as he crossed the street back to Mitzi's, but he couldn't shake the feeling he was being watched.

Colby, who was already waiting in the reptile room

when he arrived, leaned out the window to help hoist him back into the pet shop.

"Some really strange guy just walked in the front door," she whispered as she handed Tom a plastic bucket filled with everything he'd asked for. "Didn't look like he was too interested in buying a pet either."

Tom wondered if this guy and the Caddy outside were related, but he didn't want to make Colby any more nervous than she already seemed.

"What's Noodle up to?"

"Last I saw, they'd moved on to snuggling kittens. Mitzi didn't see me."

"Noodle's got the gift," said Tom, dumping almost all the springwater out the window, then spreading the rest of the ingredients in front of him. "And every good posse needs a maverick."

"How long do you think this'll take?" Colby nervously peered out the door. "That fat guy in the other room's weirding me out."

"Less than a minute. Just need to mix the vinegar with bleach to form a vitriolic solvent."

"And you know you need a three-to-one ratio of salt to acid for any vitriol compound, right?" Colby pivoted from her guarding spot near the doorway to address Tom. "I remember that from science class."

"That's the difference between you and me, Colb. You live for the A—"

"And you live for the explosion."

"True. Maybe that's why we work."

Drawing on his gloves, Tom eyeballed about twelve ounces of vinegar into the springwater jug, then sifted four ounces of powdered bleach into the solution. The surface of the bleach-green dust bubbled and smoked as it mixed into a smelly purple concoction.

"I ever tell you my dad and I developed twenty-eight different inventions using bleach?" Tom reached for the cardboard container of Comet. "Bleach hybrid battery, SuperDuperStick adhesive goop, this really cool stain remover for bicycle grease—"

"And this'll be your last invention, if we don't hurry it up," Colby interrupted. They could now hear the sound of a man's heavy shoes slowly walking the perimeter of the main room.

"Add some salt to the baking-soda-and-bleach combo, and *voilà*!" Tom began to swirl the frothing liquid inside the jug. "Homemade hydrochloric acid." He unwrapped the chocolate bar and placed it on the wooden floor, directly beneath the brick.

"Lactose and sucrose for absorption," said Colby with a nod. "Smart thinking."

"Stand back," said Tom, then carefully splashed a little bit of the acidic mixture directly onto the wall.

Hiss! Crackle!

The bricks began to dissolve, and as the excess acid dribbled down to the floor, it made contact with the candy bar, reacting with the milk and sugar to form a gummy substance that resembled a squishy putty.

"Amazing. One of your experiments could actually be working." Colby blinked.

"Gee, thanks," Tom answered, though he could hardly believe it himself. He poured a little more of the solution onto the brick.

As a small section of the wall disintegrated into a bubbling red liquid, a snug compartment behind it was exposed.

"No way." Colby rushed over, her jaw hanging open in amazement. "Are you gonna grab those already, or should I?"

"Just waiting for the acid to dry." Slowly, Tom reached

in and pulled two disk-shaped packages from the hidden space, careful not to let any exposed skin make contact with the wall.

The packages were both wrapped in brown paper. The first disk was about six inches in diameter, while the second, thicker disk was roughly half that size around. Both were covered in almost a full centimeter of gray dust.

"Unbelievable." Tom was genuinely speechless. His heart was hammering from a mixture of excitement, adrenaline, and fear.

Colby leaned forward. "What do you think they are?"

Clomp, clomp clomp clomp . . .

Heavy footfalls interrupted them. Down the hallway, but definitely getting closer to the reptile room.

In a flash, Tom stuffed the two disks into his backpack.

"Let's go!" he mouthed, leading the way as Colby followed him out the room's window. They slipped around the side of the building with only moments to spare before they heard the footsteps enter the reptile room.

"Whoever that is'll know we were there," said Colby, who was on the verge of hyperventilating. "Part of the freaking wall's dissolved."

"We can't think about that right now," said Tom. "We just have to get Noodle out of the building. I got a weird feeling about that guy."

"So do I."

The two of them went quiet, listening as the footsteps paused, paced, and paused again, probably inspecting the mess they'd left. Sweat prickled along every inch of Tom's body. There was a long silence. Perhaps the man was waiting them out. Or pulling all their fingerprints off the walls. Or loading his gun.

Finally, the footsteps headed out of the room and back down the hallway.

"Let's go back in," Tom whispered.

"Are you out of your mind?"

"Believe me, he probably thinks we're halfway to the Prospect Park subway station by now. Returning to the scene of the crime's the last thing he'd expect us to do."

"You better be right." Colby sprang to the sill and vaulted it neatly. Tom was not quite so graceful but, with Colby's help, managed to pull himself up. Crouched behind one of the largest cages, they waited until they heard the pet shop's front door slam.

Tom counted to twenty before stepping into the

hallway. "Let's hope he didn't take Noodle with him."

Out in the main room, Noodle was nonchalantly balancing a guinea pig on his head for Mitzi's amusement. He looked thrilled and relieved to see his friends.

"Took you guys long enough," he whispered to Tom. "I tried to warn you about that fat dude coming in but didn't want to blow our cover."

"It's cool. We hid from him." Tom peered through the window. The Cadillac was gone. "Did he say anything?"

"Just that he wanted to buy a kitten for his niece, but I wasn't really buying it."

"Is there a back entrance to this place?" Tom called to Mitzi, who had moved to one of the side rooms.

She seemed far more interested in the fat, yapping pug squirming and slobbering in her arms. "Helloooo, Parsley! There's a boy!"

"Another way out?" Tom asked, louder.

"There's a fire door in the back." Mitzi pointed toward the rear curtain behind her. "But I don't see why . . ." As the kids headed straight toward it, she called, "Wait! We never found your friend a dog!"

"I just remembered my mom's allergic," Noodle called back. "Sorry, Mitzi—it's been a blast!"

23
Bounce-off

Out the back door of the pet shop, Tom, Colby, and Noodle found themselves facing a pockmarked and graffitied cement wall that was way too high to climb over. Dented aluminum trash cans lined both sides of the narrow alleyway that seemed to stretch for several blocks in both directions.

"We got exactly one hour and forty minutes until curfew," noted Tom. "And this is really not a place where we want to be lost at night. Especially with some lowlife on our trail." He glanced right and left, unsure which was their best route out of there.

"Noodle, guess what? In the reptile room? We found something." Colby was still pumped up from the discovery. "Something good!"

"It better be good, considering I just spent the last twenty minutes hearing about pet psychics, while getting scratched by a buncha rodents." He showed her his arms, both red and crisscrossed with fresh claw marks.

"A small price to pay for—"

The roar of an engine interrupted her.

"*Run!*" Tom shouted as the black Cadillac came barreling down the alley, its side mirrors inches from the walls on both sides.

The car's tires screeched after them, giving chase in a streak of black tracks and sour exhaust, narrowly taking the corner that led the kids onto a small, unmarked street, then charging in their direction. Noodle was so lean and Colby so light that they could run like deer, but Tom thought his lungs would explode as his sneakers burned rubber. He was starting to regret all those times he'd skipped recess to tweak one of his robots in Dr. Kinney's wood-shop classroom.

"There's another alley!" Colby pointed to the small break in the road, twenty yards ahead of them.

"You crazy?" shouted Noodle. "Always stay on main roads when you're being chased. That way they can't corner you."

"How could you possibly know that?"

"Haven't you guys ever seen the show *Cops*? *Bad boys, bad boys, whatcha gonna do?*" he sang, then broke left and hurled a trash can directly into the car's path. The Caddy slowed to skid around it, but the can bumped and scraped against its passenger door.

Two more blocks of running, and the street finally dead-ended at a row of police barricades sectioning off what appeared to be a large street fair.

"Left, right, or lose him in the fair?" asked Noodle. There wasn't much time for hesitation, as the car was hurtling toward them at forty miles an hour and counting.

"Fair!" Tom yelled, sprinting as hard as he could to catch up.

As the three slipped underneath the barricades into the crowded street, Tom built up the nerve to glance behind him. The car had come to a halt, and leaping from it was a fat bald-headed man in a tight-fitting suit.

Tom froze in his tracks. It was the same guy he'd seen at the police station yesterday talking with Lieutenant Faber. Despite his heavy frame, the man was nimble on his feet and camouflaged himself in the crowd with surprising ease. Within seconds, there was no trace of him whatsoever.

"Noodle. Colb. We gotta hold hands," said Tom, his eyes darting at every angle. He was expecting the fat man to appear at any moment and grab them. "I know it sounds dumb, but we can't afford to get detached from one another. I have a feeling this guy's been after us for a while."

"Awesome. If I'd known I'd be chased through a street fair by a madman," said Noodle, "I might've taken a rain check on the evening portion of today's activities."

Clutching one another's sweaty hands in a daisy chain, the threesome bobbed and weaved their way through the mass of fairgoers, past the wooden stands that were brimming with pretzels, cotton candy, and homemade arts and crafts. The fair seemed to stretch for blocks on end.

"Moon bounce!" yelled Colby, suddenly spying it at the far end of the block. "That's where we want to be—somewhere public with kids, where he can't nab us without drawing attention to himself."

"We'd have to cut across the stage to get there," said Tom. "Unless we went up the block." Standing directly between them and the moon bounce was the raised platform of an outdoor theater, where actors in fluffy pink-

and-white bunny suits and yellow chick costumes were in the middle of a song-and-dance routine.

"Shortest distance between two points is a straight line!" Colby was already yanking them in the direction of the stage. Tom and Noodle had no choice but to follow as she leaped up the wooden steps, then broke hands—and Tom's rule—to race across the stage.

"Colb, wait up!" But the girl was possessed. She seemed to have shed all traces of her old overcautious, always-worried personality in favor of a gleeful daredevil Tom and Noodle could barely recognize.

"Ooph! Watch it, dude!" yelled an angry Easter Bunny as Tom accidentally knocked him into a screaming audience of delighted children.

"My fault!"

"They're ruining the show!" Parents were on their feet, and Noodle was lucky to slip out of an angry father's grip.

Across the stage, they jumped back into the crowd, but not before Tom got a second glimpse of their chubby pursuer stepping out from behind an ice-cream truck. He was a good fifty yards from them and still in dogged pursuit. But his coat was drenched in sweat now, and he was lagging. Without being spotted, Tom slipped between two old ladies and bumped through the crowd toward the moon bounce.

The threesome zigzagged past wooden stalls, heading for the inflatable room. Tom didn't even break stride as he reached into his pocket and grabbed his last dollar.

"Three tickets, keep the change, and sorry to skip the line!" he called out, then threw the bill at the ticket seller.

"Hey! You're two dollars short," the ticket seller shouted, just before the three of them disappeared into the mouth of the moon bounce.

Inside the massive plastic bubble, Colby, Tom, and Noodle blended into the cavalcade of kids bouncing around like popcorn. A chunky redhead immediately threw herself into Noodle's path. "Bounce-off!" she yelled like a sheriff out of a Western movie.

"Get away from me!" he yelled back.

"Dummy, I'm challenging you to bounce-off!" Her face was sweating red to match her hair. "Nora! Caitlyn! Come over here and help me bounce this dummy!" Two more squealing girls came springing over with a bounce intensity that sent Noodle flying up, up, and then rico-cheting against the wall.

As the girls whooped and giggled, he shot Tom a despairing look. "When's it safe to go back out there? I'm getting my skinny butt kicked like a piñata."

"I think we lost our man," Tom called back, then bounced his way to the front of the room and looked out onto the street fair. There was no sign of the fat man, which made it feel even scarier. Like he was just wait-ing to leap out from behind any food cart or cluster of people.

"Maybe we really did lose him." Colby had bounced her way to his side. "Told ya this was the place to hide." She executed a perfect somersault that caused the younger girls to oooh.

"Look! There's a side chute here," said Noodle. "We can slip out the back and lose him for sure in the food court." It seemed as good a plan as any other, and they only had another fifty-three minutes till curfew.

One by one, they vaulted back onto solid cement.

"You're right, Tom. He's nowhere," said Colby.

But as the three of them sprinted along Bedford Avenue toward the Prospect Park subway station, Tom still couldn't shake the very real, very worrisome feeling that he had now crossed way out of his safety zone.

They were messing with people way more dangerous than their parents. People with shady connections to police officers, people who spied on others from their messy cars.

But finding those two mysterious wrapped packages at Mitzi's made the treasure hunt real. Edison and the Sub Rosa were hiding something. Tom was sure of it now, and whatever that something was, he was going to find it before anyone else.

There was no turning back. He just hoped Noodle and Colby would stay with him. He couldn't finish this without them.

24
Last Resort

G old? Are you pulling my chain, Tom?" The young police commissioner sat back in his seat and exhaled long and deep.

"I'm as serious as an undertaker, Teddy," Edison answered.

He knew how crazy it must've sounded. Roosevelt was not even a year in office, and here he was, getting hit with a scientific conspiracy of global proportions.

"Tesla and I began experimenting with the dissolution of tinctures several years ago when he worked for me. It started off as a bit of fun, but . . ." Edison carefully lowered his coffee cup to its porcelain saucer and set it on the table next to him.

Aside from his wife and Tesla, of course, no one else in the world even knew about his secret basement lab, and as nervous as Edison was about bringing in another party, desperate times called for desperate measures.

He paused for another moment, gathering his thoughts before proceeding.

"Our research was going along quite well," Edison finally said, "until Nikola began on these wild diatribes about particle bombs and death rays. As we got closer to finding the alchemy formula, he became even more obsessed, until finally I had no choice. I had to stop funding the project. If we ever were to find the recipe, he simply couldn't be trusted with it."

"And how did Tesla take the news?" asked Roosevelt.

"How do you think? He went into a blinding rage, vowing to destroy my career, which I easily dismissed, of course. That is, until this detestable business with alternating currents began." Roosevelt nodded knowingly. Edison and Tesla's public feud about the future of electrical distribution was common knowledge, even to the most uninformed citizen.

"When he was just an engineer, I wasn't worried. But now with George Westinghouse in the picture, paying huge royalties for these patents, I can only fear the worst."

"So, assuming I do believe you about this alchemy business,

where do I come in?" said Roosevelt, *his brow furrowed in concentration.*

Edison couldn't help laughing. As a young army officer, Teddy had gained a reputation for his "cut to the chase" attitude, and meeting him now, Edison could see why.

"Tesla's research must be stopped. At all costs. Heaven forbid this formula gets into the wrong hands. It would be a recipe for global disaster."

"So you're saying it exists?"

Edison shifted his eyes toward the Vesper Inn's window. It was one of his favorite places in New York to grab a coffee and chat with one of the many artists who spent time there.

"I'm close," he answered. *"I may be one year away, I may be ten. But Tesla is a brilliant man, who's on a mission to find the formula . . . and destroy me."*

"Well, Mr. Edison, I'm not one for sorcery, but you have as impeccable a reputation as any man in this great country. If you say Tesla's work must be stopped, then that's all there needs to be said."

"So . . . what will you do?" Edison couldn't help a nervous quiver from entering his voice.

"The less you know, the better, sir. Now if you'll excuse me, I have a city to protect." And with that, Roosevelt shot up from his chair, spun on his polished boot, and headed toward the door.

Edison could only sit there shaking his head in disbelief. Despite the positive outcome of this meeting, he wasn't used to being spoken to so curtly. Perhaps what they said about this new commissioner was right. A career in politics might just suit him.

So that was it? Edison thought once Roosevelt had left. A snap of my fingers, and Tesla is finished?

The hard part now would be living with the guilt.

25

A Long Shot

7:04 p.m. The first day with a new curfew, and they'd already blown it.

The kitchen door flew open, and a sweating Tom raced through, heading toward the basement door with Noodle and Colby close on his heels. It felt like they hadn't stopped sprinting since Brooklyn. Even though the trip home had taken them less than two hours, it felt to Tom like a couple of lifetimes ago. The anticipation of discovering what was inside those two packages had fueled him the entire way.

Passing his dad at the kitchen table, who bounced Rose on his lap while talking on the phone and perusing a heap of bills, Tom skidded on his heels. Amid all the excitement, he'd almost forgotten that he was still in hot—if not boiling—water with his parents. Fortunately, though, his dad didn't seem to notice he'd missed curfew.

"How come you're late?" Mr. Edison glanced up from his checkbook with the phone still cradled to his ear. "I thought we had an agreement."

So much for that theory.

"We were at Colby's and lost track of time."

His dad's eyes focused on Tom, suspicious.

"It was all my fault, Mr. E," said Noodle quickly, striking the perfect chord of regretful and sweet. "I asked Tom and Colb to help me with my demo CD for that NYU summer program. Remember the one I was telling you about?"

Mr. Edison hesitated a moment, before nodding slowly. "Oh, right. I remember."

It was a perfect white lie. Specific, brief, and related to schoolish stuff, which all parents loved to hear.

"Do your mom and Colby's nana know you're both here?"

"Uh-huh," said Noodle. "They just wanted you to call and make sure it was okay." Which was true.

"All right, as soon as I'm off with these people." Tom's

dad sifted through some papers, momentarily distracted. "Yes, I'll continue to hold," he then said into the phone.

"Tommy play!" Rose held out her fat arms, and Tom scooped her up. He could never resist his sister, who smelled of equal parts applesauce, baby powder, and spit. He swung her into the air a couple of times, to her delight, then placed her on the kitchen floor, where she wobbled over to her half-finished wood-block building.

"Who're you on with?" Tom asked.

"Electric company." His dad swept the bills up into a neat stack, just out of Tom's sight line.

Leaning against the basement door were three thick piles of flattened storage boxes, which Tom slid out of the way. A depressing reminder of their impending move. Not like he needed to be reminded.

"So we're gonna go downstairs and—"

"Yes, hi, I'm still here." His father snapped to attention. "The name on the account is Thomas Edison. E-d-i-s-o-n." Pause. "I'm his great-grandson, in fact." Pause. "Sure, I guess there is a small irony to it." Pause, followed by a frustrated rub of his bloodshot eyes. "I'm hopeful that I can get this check to you by Friday, and so I really have to ask, and thanks in advance, if you'd please, please not shut off our electricity. This check is good, and I'll get it into the mail first thing in the morning. I promise."

Noodle and Colby had already headed down to the basement, but Tom remained at the top of the stairs, listening to his father's conversation from behind the half-opened door. It was awful to hear his dad plead like that.

"E-d-s-n," Rose mimicked, with a toothy grin, clapping two blocks together.

"Yes, I do realize that this is my third notice. And yes, I sincerely apologize for being so delinquent."

Tom couldn't listen anymore. Sometime during the last ten minutes, all the excitement and adventure from the afternoon had drained out of him.

As he trudged down the stairs, an inexplicable feeling came over Tom all at once, a sweat-under-the-collar charge of pure, spiky defiance. He decided he was going risk anything and do whatever it took to keep his family in Yonkers. This was their home, where they were meant to be. They were going to stay. That was that. He didn't understand why, but he had never been so sure of anything.

Down in the basement, Tom flipped on the light,

dropped his backpack onto the desk, and pulled out the two disk-shaped packages.

Together, the three of them ripped the thick brown paper from the larger disk to reveal a wax record.

"That's what you two were so excited about?" said Noodle. "An old record? I thought it was gonna be way more cool and Edison-y."

"Any century-old secret'll look a little dull and dusty at first," said Tom.

"If you say so."

Hoping for a better surprise, Noodle tore off the paper from the smaller package with a bit less reverence.

"Hmmmm." He rotated the circular metal casing. "This one's slightly more interesting." There was a small, rusty clasp along the gray case's edge, which Noodle unlocked, releasing a tiny burst of air.

Inside the case was a tightly wound roll of what appeared to be movie film. Tom grabbed it from Noodle and unspooled it up against the light.

"Do you realize we might be the only people alive to ever see this?" Goose bumps were running all along his arms as he tried to make out the small, shadowy figures imprinted on the frames.

"We're gonna need one of those old-timey projectors to watch whatever's on that film," said Colby. "Maybe we can borrow one from school."

"Or maybe there's a place to rent one?" offered Noodle.

Tom shook his head. Those options would either cost money, which none of them had, or come with too many grown-ups asking questions. Plus, somehow he knew this movie film wouldn't work on a regular projector. It felt too simple for the Sub Rosa.

"Maybe your pops can help us," added Noodle. "Scientist-wise, I mean."

"No parents," Tom snapped. "We need another game plan."

The truth was, he wanted to share this discovery with his dad more than anything, but he couldn't risk his parents ending their journey, or worse, handing these strange artifacts over to the police or a museum, neither of which could be trusted.

"No one else really uses film projectors anymore, except movie theaters." Colby stuck a pencil through the center of the record and gave it a spin. "Not to mention we need to find an antique phonograph, too."

"I *am* related to the guy who invented one of those, and I'm pretty sure I've seen some projector parts lying around here somewhere."

Tom took off to a corner of the basement lab known as the scrap heap, where everything from a barely used metronome to a collection of discarded toaster-oven coils lay in a messy heap of randomness. He immediately grabbed a kitchen funnel, a thingamabob, and a lead pipe from the pile, then tried to fit all sorts of different parts to one another—a trumpet to a pipe, a speaker to a magnet—but quickly realized none of those components were going to work. In fact, he had absolutely zero idea how to construct either a phonograph or a movie projector.

"Guess my family connection doesn't count for much," Tom admitted as he returned to the others, unable to let go of the funnel and pipe in case fleeting inspiration struck.

"What about Snert?" Colby snapped her fingers. "Not only can he fix anything, but I bet you next week's allowance he's watching a movie right now."

"Snert!" Noodle said. "He's like the original AV geek."

"Snert," Tom echoed.

Nicholas Snert. The weirdest kid in the sixth grade. He

was a year younger than Tom, Noodle, and Colby—but he was enrolled in so many advanced classes, it was like he was two grades higher. He stood on the highest plane of geekdom and collected everything from bugs to bugles. His real passion, though, was movies.

"That could be the best idea, or possibly the worst," Tom determined. "And I'm not that excited about bringing someone else in on our secret."

"Who said anything about bringing him in? We'll invite him to watch movies. We just won't tell him what kind. I say best idea," said Noodle.

"I say best, too," Colby added. "Only because we're running out of options. And time."

26

A Message from Another Country

The following morning, the round, freckled bowling ball also known as Snert was standing in the middle of Tom's basement looking like he'd just returned from a lost weekend with rogue clowns. His socks didn't match, his hair was a bird's nest, and there was a light orange film of Cheez Doodle dust on his upper lip.

On the positive side, the boy genius had made good on his promise, and a large portion of what looked to be an obsolete movie projector rested by his feet.

Snert had sounded excited when they'd spoken on the phone the night before and didn't mind interrupting his own fifteen-hour *Lord of the Rings* marathon to help out. "I've done this marathon like seven times already," said Snert. "Guess that makes me Lord of the Marathon. And

I think I can get my hands on what you're talking about. A classic Kodascope projector that could play a sixteen-millimeter reel? Yup, I just might be your man."

Tom's mom had seemed a tiny bit suspicious when Snert showed up on their doorstep right after breakfast, but once again Noodle had saved the day, informing Mrs. Edison that Snert was lending his film expertise to help them put together a music video for his NYU summer program.

"Anything to separate me from all the other bozo applicants," he'd told her.

And when Tom's mom had wondered why the three of them weren't spending their time away from school relaxing and riding bikes like all the other neighborhood kids, Noodle had responded with a sly wink. "Because all that time I spend at school is interfering with my real education, Mrs. E."

Tom couldn't tell if she'd bought his line or not, but he'd charmed her in classic Noodle style.

Now Snert was acting like he owned the place. "We'll have to make a couple of minor adjustments to this old clunker. Whip up what we don't have," he asserted, then immediately began directing the kids like a traffic cop.

"First, a base for the projector. And the stock's too wide for these spools. We'll need something to thread the film. What're ya standing around for?" His pudgy hands clapped. "We need to move, people! Time is money!"

"Snert, you might be a genius, but you're still only twelve," Colby reminded him, tweaking his ear as she passed.

Fortunately, Tom's basement was a promised land of widgets, gadgets, and discarded whatchamacallits, so even if they couldn't find the exact part Snert needed, there was always a close approximation lying somewhere nearby.

Snert showed Noodle how to feed the old film over and under four empty spools, while Colby had to glue a flashlight to the inside of the old projector to replace its gray-filmed, blown-out bulb. The phonograph, however, proved to be a much easier machine to assemble. They constructed its spinning base as a group project, by sticking a pencil through a pizza tray then hammering it to a bicycle wheel. In a final blaze of Snertspiration, the sixth-grade wonder fastened a large kitchen funnel to serve as the record player's amplifier.

It only took three hours, including a quick scramble upstairs for turkey-and-Swiss sandwiches, until the crew was ready for the Sub Rosa short film world premiere.

"We ask that you please turn off all cell phones and pagers," said Noodle, crouching behind the movie projector, his index finger positioned over one of the wooden spools that had been screwed into its side.

"What if it's, like, the first Dracula movie ever?" Snert grabbed a handful of microwave butter-flavored popcorn as Colby snapped off the overhead lights. "Like, pre-*Nosferatu*. If so, I think I deserve a distribution cut, okay?"

"How about this instead?" Noodle thwopped the back of Snert's neck. "You make me glad to be an only child."

"Okay, folks." Tom flicked on the projector's flashlight and took a seat next to Colby, while Noodle powered on the machine. They watched in silence as the film was pulled quickly past a magnifying glass that had been glued to the front of the projector to replace its cracked lens.

On the hanging white bedsheet they'd rigged up as an improvised movie screen, a blurred image took shape.

It didn't look like much of anything.

"It doesn't look like much of anything," said Tom.

"Easy fix!" Snert hopped up from his crate seat and

142

moved the magnifying glass a little farther . . . and farther from the film, until the picture on the wall slowly, wobblingly, shifted into focus.

"I see something," squeaked Colby. "Maybe. No."

"Yes, you do see something, 'cause I see it, too," said Noodle. "It's . . . two old people . . . doing some kinda waltz?"

The grainy film continued to flicker, and the image of a slender, elderly woman in a long satin ball gown and a gentleman with slicked silvery-toned hair performing a simple but graceful three-step took hold through the scratchy film.

"Who are those people?" Colby squinted. "They look like grandparents on good diets."

"Impeccable olden-days rhythm, too. I'm feelin' their groove." Noodle bopped his head in time with the silent music.

The man on the screen gave his delicate partner a final twirl, then stepped squarely in front of the camera and started to blink his eyes. As the man's face filled the screen, Tom realized he'd seen those eyes before in a photograph. They belonged to Thomas Edison's other best friend, Henry Ford.

Blink-blinkity blink. Blink. Blink blink.

Ten seconds of this, and the film cut to black. Tom stared mutely at the wall, then glanced over at Noodle, who mouthed the word *Ford* back to him excitedly.

"That's it?" Snert bounced in frustration. "Where'd you say you found this flick again?"

"The library," answered Tom at the same time that Noodle said, "Tom's attic."

"It's actually an old film from Tom's grandparents' library," said Noodle. "Or so we think."

Snert squinted, obviously not recognizing the old automobile tycoon's face. "So maybe that old dude's Thomas E the Second, huh? I guess that's cool. But when you get down to it, it's still just a boring old home movie." Snert sighed. "You shoulda told me earlier. What a gyp."

"Sorry, no Draculas for you, Snertsy." Colby offered him the rest of the popcorn as a consolation prize.

"Well, I should be getting back," he said, grabbing a handful and stuffing it into his mouth. "Aragorn and Gandalf await my hasty return!"

"Snert, as weird as you are, it was still really cool of you to help us make the projector and phonograph," said Tom. "Thanks."

"Anytime." Snert puffed up a little bit as he headed toward the stairs. He then let out a deep exhale, like he was preparing for a big race, and abruptly spun around to face the others. "Maybe I can sit with you guys at lunch one of these days."

"You got it, Snert!" Tom called back. "See ya at school."

"He's a cutie," said Colby once he was gone. "I just added him to my Top Five Sixth Graders."

"Play the movie again," said Tom, standing to face the screen.

Noodle raised his eyebrows. "Arright. But we already know the big twist at the end."

The threesome watched with razor focus as the dancers once again appeared on the bedsheet. Tom stepped closer to it and reached out to touch Ford's blinking face, casting a distorted shadow over the entire scene. Even though it was not Thomas Edison staring back at him, Tom still had never felt so close to his famous double-great-grand-father, so included in his private world. It was as if, for a moment, he had crossed space and time.

"It's deliberate, don't you think?" he turned to ask the other two.

"Duh," said Noodle. "Why would they go through so much trouble just to hide some movie of two people dancing?"

"Play it one more time," said Tom. "There's a secret here. Has to be."

He stared as if hypnotized by Ford's blinking eyes. The film reached its conclusion, then cut to black.

"Again," Tom repeated.

"Let me save you the suspense," Noodle quipped. "Dance dance dance. Blink blink blink. It's not gonna be any different." But he reset the film anyway and started it one more time.

Tom was at a loss as he studied every inch of the dancers, as well as the wooden wall behind them, the crystal chandelier hanging above their heads. No detail was too insignificant.

Three more viewings, and he was no closer to an answer. In fact, he didn't even know what he was supposed to be looking for.

Maybe the answer's on the record, he thought, and was about to suggest they play the phonograph when Colby shot up from her crate.

"I got it!"

"What?" Tom turned to face her. "What've you got?"

"It's Morse code! Good ole Ford's trying to blink a message to us!"

"Ha! I knew one day I'd regret not joining Boy Scouts," said Noodle.

"Someone grab a laptop and download the Morse code alphabet."

"I'm on it!" Noodle flew up the stairs, while Tom cued up the film projector. Colby plucked Tom's notebook off the table and scrounged around for something to write with.

"Play it again." She sat with a pencil poised as soon as Noodle returned with his MacBook in hand.

Unbeknownst to the three of them, hidden within the shadows beneath Tom's worktable, a tiny red light blinked away, the only sign of the listening device that had been secretly planted there the night before. Steadily, it blinked. On and off. Recording everything it heard.

27
The Waltz

That's an *N*. And the last one's an *E*, I think."

Colby finally looked up from her notebook. Her weary eyes were starting to sting from exhaustion. Noodle, too, raised his long arms above his head and stretched. He'd been hunched over his laptop for each one of the seventy-six Sub Rosa film viewings that it had taken to decipher Ford's blinking, and now his neck and back felt like an eighty-year-old arthritic's.

Like a drone, Tom rewound the film and replayed the movie for the seventy-seventh time that afternoon.

"Yep. Definitely an *E*," said Colby.

"So what've we got?" Tom asked.

She held her notebook to her face, squinting to read her

hastily drawn letters. "M-L-E-9-E-N-L-A-C-I-K-A-W-N-A-A-L-N-I."

"Great. More Sub Rosa gibberish." Noodle let out a frustrated sigh as he tilted dangerously far back on his crate seat. "Why can't he just say, 'All the gold's buried under the pet shop's porch? Bring a couple suitcases.'"

Colby remained silent, shaking her head every so often as she continued to stare at her notebook. "There's some pattern here, I know it. I'm just not seeing it."

Tom knew that if there was some kind of hidden mathematical formula, Colby was their only shot at finding it, and the best way to help her was by keeping quiet and staying out of her way.

"Noodle, you ready for the next piece?" said Tom, carefully removing the record from its paper casing. Using only the edges of his hands to hold it, he dropped the antique record onto the mounted pizza tray, then gave the whole delicate contraption a whirl. As the record spun, Tom lowered the phonograph's bent-sewing-needle arm onto the waxy grooves of the spinning record.

Within seconds, the tinny, scratchy sound of an orchestra filled the basement. Then, wafting high above the horn section, they heard a man's lilting tenor.

"Ugh, sounds like the music Nana plays when it's bridge night at my house." Colby glanced up from her notebook long enough to wrinkle her nose.

"Shh." Noodle put his finger to his lips as the man on the record continued to sing. *"My whisper takes you to the place, I'm right below your feet. So hop on board the railway cart to find our secret suite—"*

Suddenly the record lurched, momentarily cutting off the music, before skipping backward.

"My whisper takes you to the place . . . My whisper takes you to the place . . . ," the man sang over and over and over again.

Noodle lifted the needle off the record. "Three-quarter time. Heavy string section. Classic, no-frills waltz."

"Fascinating," said Tom. "Who cares?"

"You should!" Noodle gave his friend a good, hard whack on the arm. "Because those two in the movie? They're also dancing a waltz."

"So it's a coincidence?"

"What would you two do without me?" Noodle closed his eyes as if he were trying to explain calculus to a toddler, savoring the moment. It was one of the rare times when he had the answer to a puzzle, and Tom and Colby didn't. "You both are really lucky, you know that? That I've decided to take time out of my busy schedule to help guide you—"

"Noodle, O great genius of the Sub Rosa, please just tell me why the song's important before I kill you."

"It's easy. The music's the soundtrack for the movie!"

"Oh. Right." Tom looked a little bit let-down. "I would've figured that out eventually."

"We'll never know, will we?"

Together, the two of them cued up the phonograph and projector.

"I knew you two'd manage on your own," said Colby from across the room.

"How's it coming over there?" Tom looked over, but Colby's face was again burrowed in her notebook.

"Just trial and error at this point. I'll either get it in ten minutes or ten weeks."

"The first one would be preferable."

"Ready, T? All together now, and a-one, and a-two . . ." Like a maestro at Carnegie Hall, Noodle gave the cue to synchronize the image and sound, then stood back and watched as the orchestral music on the record lined up perfectly with the dancing.

And just like before, the record skipped again as Ford pivoted to the camera and started to blink. Seconds later, the film cut to black while the music quietly repeated over and over.

"Probably ninety years too late to get our money-back guarantee," said Noodle as he blew some dust off the record, then lifted it close to his nose to inspect for any unseen scratches.

"Unless it's skipping on purpose," said Tom. "It seems like the skip begins right as Henry starts to blink. But what that's all about, I have no idea. . . ." His sigh echoed the others' frustration. "And I have no idea what the secret suite, or whisper or any of it means."

"I cracked the code!" Colby shot a triumphant fist into the air, scribbling letters as fast as she could. "It was a simple cipher, actually. Following the equation, n equals n plus four divided by n. Each letter in the alphabet of course corresponds with a number. A is one. B is—"

"Colb!" Noodle yelled. "Once again. Stop geeking out. Just tell us what it says."

"Mile Nine. Lackawanna Line!"

"What's that?" said Tom. "Like a railroad line?"

Colby shrugged her shoulders as Noodle hopped back to his laptop and began typing away. Within a couple of moments, he had an answer.

"Bingo! The Lackawanna Line was an old rail line that used to run out of Union Square into Jersey. Till the nineteen fifties, when the Hudson and Manhattan Railroad went bankrupt, and then it became the PATH train."

"How far away is it?"

"Well, basically it just follows the Newark PATH line, but I don't know where mile nine would be. Somewhere in Jersey, I guess."

"When's the last train to Newark tonight?"

"Whoa, Tom—slow your roll," Colby interrupted. "We all wanna find the Sub Rosa treasure, but what about our parents and—"

"We'll make up excuses or wait till they go to bed. Or I'll go by myself." Tom's voice had pitched louder without his even realizing it. "I'm not too chicken to check out a train track after hours."

"No one said you were." Noodle put up his hands. "We're not the enemy, remember? And we still got a couple more days of spring break left to figure this out."

"We can't wait another day," said Tom. "Solving this thing's our only chance to stay together."

"But none of that will matter if we get busted for sneaking out," said Colby.

"Then you guys can bail if you want!"

Tom could feel himself getting emotional and angry at his friends for no reason, but the truth was, he was terrified to go to New Jersey without Noodle and Colby. He needed them. Who would sweet-talk a police officer if they got busted? Or crack whatever math equation or lock combination was awaiting them at the next hiding spot?

Scared as he was, Tom's mind was made up. Nothing was going to keep him from saving the family's name and fulfilling his destiny.

"Wherever this Lackawanna Line is, I'm going there. Tonight," he heard himself say, pretending to have a lot more confidence than he felt. "Are you guys with me or not?"

He looked to Noodle, then Colby. The wait was painful, as neither of them said a word.

"Because I don't think I can do this on my own," Tom finally admitted.

154

28
Up in Flames

Gloved hands splashed gasoline over every inch of the dark basement, pouring it onto the piles of books and papers, dusty furniture, even the wheelbarrow and cracked flower pots that were in storage until the summer. It was March, which meant the air was wet and cold, so it would take a lot of gas to do the job right.

The man stood there in silence, surveying the damage. A few days ago, when he'd received an anonymous call offering him five hundred dollars to torch the entire structure, he'd happily complied. It was pretty simple work. Get in, get out. Get the cash.

As to what he was destroying—nah, he didn't want to know. Better if he didn't. It was a job. Nothing more.

The match sparked in his freezing hands, and within seconds, the whole space was doused in dancing yellow light. Without even pausing to admire his work, the man climbed up through the sidewalk hatch and disappeared down a side street and into the night.

The flames licked higher, devouring the paper and exploding toward the ceiling. In minutes, it had spread upward, all the way to the building's second floor.

Outside, panicked gawkers, their coats and mufflers pulled hastily over their flannel nightgowns, had begun to spill into the sidewalks. Moments later, wailing fire engine sirens whined down the street, and whoever wasn't awake yet was now.

Horse-drawn and steam-powered, the fire trucks rolled heavily up to the house. Uniformed firemen rolled out their hoses to battle the flames.

As he turned the corner onto Fifth Avenue, his eyes and ears still rapt from an evening out at the theater, it took Nikola Tesla several moments to register exactly what was going on. Even as he heard the sirens and caught the smell of smoke, a thick current in the cold night air, he never could've imagined that the cause of all the commotion was his very own building, and even as he stood in front of the blazing block, he needed a few moments to register what was happening.

Edison.

It was all Tesla could think as he raced up to one of the overseeing police officers, grabbing fistfuls of the man's uniform as he swung him around by his arms. "I know who did this! Do you hear me? I will demand restitution!" His eyes brimmed.

And I will have my revenge, he vowed silently.

The police officer unclasped Tesla's hands. "Mr. Tesla, would you mind answering some questions for us?" The officer spoke slowly as he attempted to escort the shaking inventor away from the fire, to safety. But within a few paces, Tesla broke free from his grasp, collapsing onto the curb in front of the burning building. Let the fire take him, too. He was nothing without his work. Those papers, all that data—it represented years of his life, his best research, his most inspired thought. Without his lab, who was he?

He was ruined—by Thomas Edison.

29
The Great Escape

The digital clock on Tom's bedside table read 10:16. His parents had only gone to bed fifteen minutes ago, but in order to catch the 10:31 Metro-North out of Yonkers, he would have to leave now.

Quietly, Tom rolled out from under his comforter, fully dressed in black like a ninja. The computer printouts, extra pens and notepads, a triple-sealed plastic bottle of hydrochloric acid, two steel shovels, a mallet, and one chisel had already been stuffed into a duffel bag under his bed. Tom had no idea what was waiting for him at mile nine, but whatever it was, he figured he was probably going to have to dig, hammer, or burn his way through something sturdy to get to it.

He held his breath as he slid the heavy duffel bag out into the open, careful not to let the shovels clank against each other.

"Phase one complete," Tom mumbled to himself.

Phase two: escape.

Tiptoeing toward the bedroom door, he opened it an inch at a time, braced for any telltale whispering or rustling from his parents' bedroom, but all he could hear were the faint sounds of the local TV news coming through their door.

Then, with his shoes in hand and the duffel bag slung over his shoulder, he stepped into the upstairs hallway.

All night, Tom had been at the computer, researching the history of the New York railroad system. As his bedtime came and went, he could feel the scratch behind his eyelids and the heaviness in his bones. He'd have to keep his wits sharp tonight, and that wouldn't be easy.

Though the Edison family's narrow Victorian home had a back staircase, a hidden ladder, a gabled attic, a basement plus root cellar, and a functioning dumbwaiter, the one thing it didn't have was an easy escape route. There was no sturdy ledge under Tom's bedroom window, and it was a good twenty-foot free fall to the street. The only ways out were the obvious routes: front door or kitchen door. Tom chose the front.

It took him a full three minutes to creep down the main stairs. After each creak or squeak, he'd catch his breath, frozen in the darkness, praying he hadn't tipped off his parents, who were probably just dozing off right about now. The living room was a minefield of half-packed boxes, furniture, book piles, and the most dangerous obstacles of all, Rose's strewn toys. One false move would send Tom crashing to the ground for sure.

After what felt like six lifetimes, he finally reached the front door, stepping through and locking it ever so gently behind him. Outside, the neighborhood was settling down for the night. All along the line of modest homes, lights were being snapped off and doors bolted.

As he continued along the sidewalk, all Tom could hear was the mosquito-like buzz from the streetlights. But no sign of life. Once he'd reached the end of the block, he was welcomed by darkness. And then . . .

Blink, blink, blink the flashlight signaled in the distance.

Tom practically keeled over with relief as he darted

across the street to where Noodle and Colby were crouched behind a row of shrubs, waiting for him.

Like Tom, they were dressed head to toe in black and, like Tom, they both looked sleepy and nervous all at once.

"Ready?" he asked, his breath cold in the sharp spring air.

"Yup. Let's do this." Noodle adjusted his black baseball cap low over his eyes as they headed in the direction of the Yonkers train station.

Their journey to Hoboken was complicated, with three transfers each way and little room for error. If they missed a single connection, if one subway or train was more than five minutes late, the entire plan would unravel, and they'd be busted for sure.

Tonight would actually be the second time the three of them had pulled an all-nighter. The last one was on Halloween, also the same night as Colby's thirteenth birthday. Noodle had decided it would be fun to watch six straight hours of zombie movies to see how scared they could get. Sure enough, all of them had made it to see the sunrise, simply because they'd been too terrified to fall asleep.

"According to my research," Tom informed them as they jogged toward the station, "the Lackawanna Line was one of the first interstate railroads ever to have originated out of New York City."

"And by my math," added Colby, "mile nine, on the old route, will put us a ways away from the riverfront. Somewhere between Palisades and Central Avenue."

As they turned onto Buena Vista Avenue, Noodle was the first to see the Metro-North train pulling into the station.

"Wait!" he yelled as the three of them started sprinting. "Hold that train!"

The brakes swooshed to a stop as Tom reached the station. The heavy duffel bag knocked hard against his legs, slowing him down, as Noodle and Colby slipped into the departing train.

"Come on!" they yelled.

Tom dashed onto the platform, heaving his bag between the train's closing doors. Once it began pulling out of the station, Tom had to run to keep up with it—but he couldn't get through the doors.

"Hit the emergency brake!" Tom yelled.

"We got it," Noodle called back, as he and Colby

162

pulled on the doors with all their strength, securing it open by two inches.

If he didn't go for it now, he'd miss the train. Tom inhaled and lunged at the door. He got his torso through, but the doors locked around his waist like a mechanical shark.

"Hold on!" Colby commanded as she and Noodle each grabbed one of Tom's hands and pulled him in the rest of the way.

Fifteen minutes into the night's adventure, and they'd almost tripped up at the gate.

They collapsed into the train's vinyl seats. Colby couldn't help laughing. "At least now we're all wide awake."

30
Welcome to Hoboken

Anyone else having second thoughts about the intelligence of this plan?" asked Noodle, speaking for all of them as their flashlights cut through the deserted railroad tracks that stretched from the Hoboken waterfront. In the distance, a car siren wailed, startling a pack of dogs. Their collective barking filled the night.

"Just keep your eyes peeled," said Colby. "That's what my nana always says." Her own eyes were round as saucers.

As they continued along the railroad tracks, Colby knelt down and used her flashlight to check over her notebook calculations, which seemed to indicate that they were somewhere between miles seven and eight on the old Lackawanna Line.

"And what is it we're looking for, again?" asked Noodle.

"Not sure," said Tom. "I'm hoping we'll know it when we see it."

"Could it be this?" Noodle's flashlight illuminated a weatherworn white stone marker with the words MI 7 etched in faint block letters.

"Mile seven!" Tom exclaimed. "It must be left over from the original railroad."

"Good. So we're close. Ish," said Colby.

"It'd still be nice to know what we're close to." Noodle slowly swept his flashlight back and forth in front of them, roving the area like a metal detector.

But there was fresh energy in their steps as they upped the pace along the tracks. After another mile, the dark shadows of a large structure began to take form in the far-off distance.

"Tunnel ahead." Colby motioned to it once she was able to make out its gaping diameter tucked underneath a tree-lined hill.

"I really hope we get to marker nine before we get to the mouth of that thing," said Noodle. "Doesn't seem to be a lot of wiggle room in there."

"Well, there's mile marker eight," said Tom as his flashlight landed on it. They were still several hundred yards away from the tunnel, but it was looking bad, because the track they'd been following from the train station disappeared into a narrow mouth.

"Marker nine's gotta be in there somewhere," said Tom moments later, when they finally arrived at the tunnel's opening.

They stopped, uncertain. On both sides, there was no more than a foot of space between the edge of the railroad tracks and the wall.

"Any last words?" gulped Noodle, peering forward into the shadows.

"Yeah, how about, I hope I don't get hit by a train?" Colby reflexively glanced behind. In the hour or so that they'd been walking, only one single, tired old freight had chugged past, but none of them wanted to get stuck inside that tunnel if and when the next one decided to come along.

"Let's have some faith. Please." Tom was busy prying open a metal box affixed to the side of the tunnel's entrance, just beneath a small traffic light. "Hold my flashlight?" As Noodle grabbed for it, Tom explained,

"My dad once told me these stoplights run on timers, so trains can only enter the tunnel when the light's green. If I can somehow rejigger it . . . "

He opened the well-rusted metal box to reveal the light's circular mechanized timer inside. It made a faint buzzing sound as a gray disk slowly counted off the seconds. Tom folded up two pieces of loose-leaf paper from Colby's notebook and wedged them into the timer's gears.

"Ya know, most kids' dads teach them how to throw a football when they're growing up," said Noodle.

"Well, mine taught me how to trip-wire our home security system." Tom watched as the tunnel's traffic light changed from green to red. "Not that there's ever anything at my house worth stealing."

"So how much time do we have?" Colby could feel her insides twisting from nerves, but she was determined to be brave.

"As long as we need. I've blocked the timer, so the light won't turn green. But we should still try and get out of here as soon as possible."

"Ya think so, genius?" said Noodle as the three of them stepped inside the tunnel's all-encompassing blackness.

Even their flashlights provided only weak patches of illumination in the dark.

Whoosh! Tom and Noodle turned at the sound of Colby's inhaler, followed by the sound of her sneakers squeaking against the rusted railroad tracks as she followed them in.

"What happened to Colby the daredevil from the other day?" asked Noodle.

"Hey, two days ago, you wouldn't have even been able to get me on the Metro-North."

31
MI 9

Their flashlights darted like dragonflies, sweeping and lighting different sections of a damp, crumbling wall, momentarily illuminating graffiti and leaky pipes that crisscrossed paths along the ceiling.

"It smells like feet and mushrooms in here," said Noodle.

"No, it smells like vinegar and cat farts," corrected Colby.

"No. Actually it smells like old tin—"

"Guys, enough!" Tom barked. "We need to concentrate right now."

"Sor-*ry*, grumpy old man," said Noodle as Colby suppressed a chuckle.

Together, they walked along in silence; the echoing

drip-drop of water splashing onto the tracks provided a haunting background noise.

Tom hadn't meant to snap, but finding Edison's treasure—or lost invention or whatever it was—had consumed him to the point where it was impossible to joke around.

"Hey, guys." Noodle's hushed voice broke the silence. "What are you gonna tell everyone at school when they ask what you did over spring break?"

"Probably easier to lie and just say I watched DVDs with Nana."

Tom smiled ruefully. "I don't think this is what Phelps had in mind when he told me to reflect on my future."

Their laughter bounced along the concrete walls, the sound reverberating into spooky, ghoulish noises. Maybe he hadn't completely lost his sense of humor after all.

"*Woo-hoot!*" Noodle spun around. "Listen to that. We sound like a gallery of ghosts trying to—*ooomph*!" The flashlight flew from his hand and clattered to the tracks as Noodle went down with a thud.

"Noodle! Are you hurt?" Colby spun on her sneaker to find him lying flat, wincing in pain as he struggled for breath.

"Uh, I think I broke my coccyx," he moaned. "What is a coccyx, anyway?"

Tom dropped to his knees, beaming his light onto Noodle's back at the point where he clutched at it with both hands.

Next to Noodle's shoe, something white peeked up at a right angle from beneath the gravel.

"You're a genius." Tom began to scoop away some of the rocks from around the white stone. "I think you tripped on something good."

"Hey, don't worry about me dying over here. As long as I tripped on something good."

Ignoring him, Tom pulled a shovel from the duffel bag and started to dig furiously through the rocks. In a few quick turns, he had exposed the rest of another white mile marker, with MI 9 chipped into the stone.

"Just like the other two," said Colby softly.

Tom wiped his brow. "Grab a shovel and get digging."

Noodle hopped up, his coccyx miraculously repaired, and soon he and Tom were winging clumps of dirt and rock over their shoulders.

After several fruitless minutes had passed, however,

Noodle's spirits and strength began to flag.

"We got nothing but a big ole pile of gritty rubble on one side, and a big ole hole on the other," said Noodle, passing his shovel to Colby. "Thanks for the exercise in futility, T.E. the First."

"Could we have messed up the Morse code or something?" Colby began to dig alongside Tom. "Maybe I got the cipher equation wrong."

"Seems unlikely," said Noodle. "Since you're the first kid ever to have a hundred and four average in Mr. Farrell's math class."

"Guess I have to agree with your logic on that one."

Tom's shovel flew faster, his digging growing desperate.

No, no, no, he thought with every mound of overturned earth. No, they hadn't got the code wrong. The clue had to be here somewhere. They'd come too far—

"Uh-oh!" Noodle's exclamation broke Tom's thoughts. "This might put a damper on our plans!" They followed his finger toward the growing circle of light that was slowly moving its way down the tunnel toward them.

"Yikes," breathed Colby. "I thought you said no trains could come in when the light's red."

But Tom had no time to think about what had gone wrong because at that same moment his shovel clanked against a hard object.

"Wait—I got something!"

32
The Mystery Toaster Oven

W hat you got is thirty seconds!" Noodle shouted. "That train sees us, but it doesn't look like it's stopping anytime soon."

The train's whistle sounded through the darkness, its brakes shrieking as a warning light flashed several times at the kids.

Tom dropped to a crouch. "It's some kind of container." His hands pawed at the dirt. The battered and rusty tin box peeking out was roughly the size of a toaster oven, and it wasn't coming loose very easily.

"Tom! We're not waiting for you!" yelled Colby. "If we don't start running, we'll be flattened!"

Noodle was pulling at Tom's jacket. "We'll come back for it."

"It's almost loose! I'm so close." He yanked with every ounce of strength, losing balance and falling backward as it finally dislodged.

Tucking the metal box under his arm like a fullback, he took off after the others down the center of the railroad tracks. The shrill whistle and howling brakes continued ringing through Tom's ears, but he kept his eyes focused on the tunnel's opening, now only fifty feet away.

"Aaagh!" Tom felt his leg buckle as he fell to the ground, and the metal box flew from his hands. Although he couldn't see anything, he could feel his shoelace stuck on one of the track's wooden cross ties. He heard Colby's voice in the distance as he freed himself.

"Tom, hurry!"

Behind him, the train roared like a diesel-fueled beast. With no time to recover the box, and no alternate escape, he flattened himself on the tracks and offered up a quick prayer.

The train bore down, gears grinding, its tons of steel inches from his head. The sound was a deafening explosion. Nerves raw, heart pounding like a jackhammer, Tom squeezed his eyes shut as the interminable train whined and rattled above his body for what felt like an eternity.

And then, silence. The noise had stopped.

Tom peeked up to see one of the car's lower axles above his head. With shaking hands, he crawled toward the edge of the tracks.

"Please tell me you're all right!"

His ears were still numb and ringing, so it took him a second to make out Colby's voice, and then the faint outline of her face as she appeared in front of him, crouched alongside one of the train's still wheels.

"Thank God you're still three-dimensional," she said when she saw him.

Noodle and Colby each held out a hand and pulled Tom out from under the train and onto his feet.

Too shocked to speak, he leaned against his friends as they all flattened their bodies sideways to give themselves enough room to exit the tunnel.

Once out, their eyes quickly adjusted to the weak moonlight. Where the one entrance to the tunnel had been all industrial buildings, the other end offered a landscape that was thick with overgrown trees and weeds.

The front of the train was a couple hundred yards away, which made it impossible to see in the night.

"I bet there's a conductor on his way toward us right now," said Noodle. "With loads of questions."

"Wait, we almost forgot the box," Tom croaked, and was about to turn around and head back into the tunnel when—

"You kids lost or something?" The words, spoken in a heavy Brooklyn accent, fell like an anvil on the moment.

They froze. A heavyset shadow stepped out of the trees and directly in between the kids and an escape route. "Thought you lost me in Brooklyn, didn't you?"

And as his face came into the moonlight, they could see exactly who this man was.

"Pet store guy," whispered Noodle. *"Go!"*

They ran, fresh energy surging through Tom's veins. But he'd made it only a few yards before he heard a commotion and looked back to see the worst: the pet store guy had Colby by the leg.

"I didn't do anything!" she hollered.

Tom and Noodle dove into a heavy cluster of bushes and slid in the dirt.

"What do we do?" Noodle's eyes were sheer panic.

Tom's mind was awhirl. "Let me go back for her. But the metal box is still in the tunnel—"

"Yeah! Under a freaking train!"

"You have to go grab it and hide it someplace safe."

"No way I'm leaving you two! The conductor'll probably be here any second."

"Noodle, whoever that guy is, he doesn't want Colb. He wants the clue!"

"But we should all stick together—"

"That box might be exactly what we need to trade for Colby! As long as you don't get seen by anybody."

There was no point arguing. Tom was already on his feet, running back toward the fat man, who was now grappling Colby tight against his waist.

"I'll stay with her, Noodle!" Tom called over his shoulder. "Promise!"

33

The Man Behind the Screen

Let's go. Keep it moving, you two."

The fat man in the cheap suit shoved Tom and Colby up a long flight of stairs. He was huffing loudly behind them. With each exhale, Tom almost gagged from the instant coffee-and-nicotine stench.

The two of them had spent the last hour and a half in a window-blacked van, only to arrive at some enormous Manhattan brownstone that on the inside resembled a hunting lodge from another century. Mounted elk and bear heads peered down from the corridor walls, and several of the rooms they'd passed through were hung with old oil paintings of grim, ringleted ladies and equally somber ruffle-collared gentlemen.

The fat man had herded them through a few of these

more public rooms, then up a back staircase and down a narrow hallway, which finally led to a planked oak door that was on its own private landing and seemed to be secured off from the rest of the house.

The fat man gave three loud knocks on the door.

"Send them in, Nicky," came an icy voice from the other side.

The fat man turned the knob and prodded Tom and Colby into an immaculate state-of-the-art office, which looked like the bridge of a spaceship. Multiple wall-mounted monitors scrolled international stock tickers and news programs, and every piece of pristine furniture was designed in chrome and leather.

From behind his metal-and-glass desk, a wiry man gazed at Tom with a face devoid of any expression. From his slicked, silver hair to his starched white pajamas and black silk robe, he was well groomed to the point of obsession.

As Tom took another step into the room, he noticed several sheets of paper with the Alset Energy letterhead stacked near the edge of the silver-haired man's desk.

What does all this have to do with dad's old company? he wondered.

"Well, if it isn't the heir to the great Edison legacy,"

said the man. There was something disdainful about the way he'd enunciated Tom's last name. As if he'd meant it to be a punch line. But Tom was used to people saying his name like that.

"Who are you?" Tom asked.

"Someone who's been keeping close tabs on your family." The man rose from behind his desk in slippered feet and crossed the room to a small bar trolley, where he snapped open two old-fashioned glass Coke bottles and handed them to Tom and Colby. "I think it's fate that you and I are meeting now, Tom. Imagine my surprise when I learned that the boy who broke into my museum exhibit also happened to be the son of one of the lowly engineers I'd just laid off."

Tom's knees nearly collapsed from under him. He'd never even seen a photo of Curt Keller, yet the man was the reason so much had gone wrong in his life.

"What do you want from my family?" he asked. But as Keller turned, reaching for his remote to change the channel on his flat-screen, the answer became clear. Arranged neatly on the table behind his desk were all the clues they'd found so far: the wax record, the movie film, the Firestone photo. All on obvious display.

"There's nothing to fear from us, kids. I'm just taking a few necessary precautions." Keller allowed himself a tight-lipped, joyless smile. "We only intend to hold you here until Grandpa Edison's formula is safely in my hands."

Tom tried not to let the shock appear on his face. *What else* did *this guy know?*

"Now is there anything more you'd like to tell me?" asked Keller. "Something else you've found?"

"We didn't find anything," said Tom, trying to keep his voice from rising. "Our search was a dead end."

Keller leaned in close. Unlike fat Nicky's breath, his smelled like mentholated cough drops, and his bloodshot eyes seemed to look both past and through Tom.

"I can read people better than a polygraph machine," he hissed, "and you're not exactly someone I'd call a practiced liar."

Tom went silent, hoping Keller wasn't close enough to hear his heart beating like crazy.

"Really, though, I should be thanking you kids." Keller returned to his desk, where he picked up the wax record, spinning it in the edges of his hands. "As you know, my company's had a rough few years, with alternative energy sources cutting into my profits." Keller now turned his attention to the Firestone photo, inspecting it casually. "But what's a couple million when you've got the formula to make gold, right?"

This time his laugh was genuine, and it took every ounce of restraint for Tom not to lunge over and snatch the clues right out of his bony hands.

"My great-great-grandfather hid his secret specifically to keep it from people like you."

At that, Keller's face tightened, defensive as a closed fist. "Don't get started with me, son. The brilliant Thomas Edison also ruined a great many lives."

"What did he ever do to you?" asked Tom. He could feel Colby's hand on his sleeve.

"Tom, pick your fights. Trust me, this isn't one of them," she whispered. He could see something was troubling her.

Keller regarded the two of them coolly. The calmness in his blue eyes made him seem that much more terrifying.

"No, no. I'm happy to tell you." Keller smiled. "The story's quite simple, actually. Your great-great-grandpa destroyed the career of the modern era's greatest inventor, then robbed him of the credit he deserved."

"That's a lie." Tom knew his double-great-grandfather's life better than any of his history teachers, and if there was a bitter feud he'd ever had with a rival scientist, Tom certainly would've read something about it.

"I will do whatever it takes to restore my great-grandfather's name and bring the formula back into my family. Where it's always belonged." Keller tipped back in his chair as he made a dismissive sweep of his hand. "I'm afraid our visiting hour is over," he said with a glance toward Nicky, who'd been glowering in the corner of the office the entire time. "Please show our guests to their luxury suite."

Keller swiveled his body back to his desktop computer as Nicky grabbed each of the kids by an elbow, then unceremoniously marched them toward the door and out of the office.

34
The Luxury Suite

There was nothing luxurious about the luxury suite. Tom and Colby saw that right away as Nicky escorted them down two flights of stairs, then locked them into the dark, dingy room, somewhere deep within the mansion's basement. A clunky armoire and a rusty, cracked metal cot with a bare mattress were its only furnishings.

Once the fat man was out of earshot, Tom started to pace the room nervously, tapping the walls and listening for hollow points.

"Tom, what are we gonna do?" Panic crept into Colby's voice as she dropped down onto the cot, which caused it to collapse on the floor with a crash.

"You okay?" Tom turned from checking the armoire's drawers and ran to her side.

"Yeah. The mattress softened the fall."

"I'll get us out of here, Colb," said Tom, then went back to checking the room for any grates or drains. "It looks like they've got us in some kind of old servants' quarters."

"My nana's gonna be up in two hours." Colby slumped forward and stared down at the cracked cement floor. Just thinking about her poor, worried-sick nana calling the police made her nauseous. "If she's not already."

It didn't take much longer for Tom to realize that the only way out of this room was through the door. Which was bolted shut.

After a moment, he sidled up next to Colby on the mattress.

"Maybe Keller will let us go," he said weakly.

"I don't think so." Colby was shaking her head slowly. "I couldn't help noticing that the word *Alset*? Is just *Tesla* spelled backward. Like Nikola Tesla."

Tom cocked his head. "That can't be a coincidence, right? I mean, he kept talking about restoring his great-grandfather's reputation."

At the sound of Tesla's name, Tom did recall reading

something once about a professional rivalry between the two inventors, but there was obviously something more personal to it.

Colby snuck a quick hit off her inhaler. Even though it hadn't worked for years, she needed some kind of security blanket right now. "So maybe Edison and this Tesla dude had a falling-out over the formula, and now Keller wants it back in his family."

"And if Keller is Tesla's great-grandson," said Tom, "it must've made it that much sweeter for the old jerk to fire my dad."

"And one more reason he's not letting us go anytime soon."

Tom dropped his face into his hands and tried to rub the stinging sleep out of his eyes as the full reality of their hopeless situation came crashing down.

"Everything's gonna be fine," he said, though it was more to comfort himself than anything.

Colby leaned closer and rested her head on his shoulder. "I'm really gonna miss you next year, Tom."

He could feel the edge of his nose twitch, and his eyes well up. This wasn't how he'd imagined the adventure ending. Locked in some rich guy's basement, waiting for him to steal the formula from Tom's family and force them to leave New York.

Once again, he'd taken things too far. He'd gotten so wrapped up with saving his family that he'd forgotten all about their feelings. His parents had enough stress right now without a kidnapped son.

How could he have been so thoughtless?

"I guess the Edison men are just a buncha losers," said Tom with a long, defeated exhale.

"Don't be an idiot." Colby's sneaker dug into a loose mattress seam and ripped its stitching a tiny bit. "You're probably the smartest guy I know."

"Then how come I'm rocking a C average in school, and every invention I ever build ends up either blowing up or falling apart?"

"That would be because you lose interest in stuff before you ever see anything through."

It hurt Tom to admit it, but the girl had a point. It was what every teacher had been telling him since he could remember, and it was why he currently held the Saint Vincent's Academy record for most trips to Headmaster

Phelps's office in a year. He loved the rush of inspiration more than the labor of planning or studying.

Neither of them spoke for a while, and for some unknown reason Tom couldn't stop staring at Colby's sneaker. The hole she'd ripped through the mattress seam was now twice the size it had been. His eyes then caught pieces of broken cot scattered around them.

There has to be a way out, he thought. *Every problem has a solution.*

He just had to slow down and think it through for once.

For an hour, Tom stared blankly at the wall while Colby managed a few moments of sleep.

And then, somewhere around five a.m., inspiration struck.

"If I could reassemble the cot," he mumbled quietly to himself, "we could use the weight of the falling armoire to tighten..." His voice trailed off as his brain built momentum. And then...

"Colby, I've got it!" He bolted to his feet as she woke with a gasp. "This time, I'm seeing something through to the very end."

"I know that face." Colby frowned as she blinked the tiredness from her eyelids. "What completely scary task does this involve me doing?"

"You'll see." Tom began to rip one long seam of the cot's worn covering. "Eh. It's not giving."

"Here. Let me help." Colby took a step close to him, her exhaustion forgotten, ready to play her part as a new plan began to take shape.

35
Separated

Everyone's face was sick with worry, and all of them silently blamed one person.

Noodle.

Tom's parents, Noodle's mom, and Colby's nana had been called into the Yonkers Police Station when Tom and Colby hadn't returned by morning, but what was even worse was that Lieutenant Faber had somehow been tipped off to what happened, and for nearly an hour, the stern-faced police officer had grilled Noodle about his story, forcing him to retrace every detail again and again. With a sinking heart, he had come clean. He had to. Colby and Tom were missing, and he needed to do everything he could to help get them back safe.

The others had listened, stunned, as Noodle described

the Firestone photo, the short film, the fat guy from the pet shop who'd kidnapped Colby—and probably now had Tom, too. He'd kept one detail to himself, though. He wouldn't say a word about the metal box—which, at this moment, was hidden deep inside his clothes hamper—until he could have a word with Tom's dad alone.

"So. It's not a history project. It's a treasure hunt," Lieutenant Faber concluded once he'd finished.

"A really important, and now possibly extremely dangerous one," Noodle added.

"But you don't even know what kind of treasure you're looking for." Her eyebrows were arched and her mouth curled as if he'd just told her a really corny joke.

"Well, Tom thinks that the Sub Rosa's trying to protect some secret from falling into the wrong hands. And that it's up to us to find it before the bad guys."

"The bad guys. Oookay." Faber glanced at her notes, barely listening to Noodle's story. "And you think that this abductor is after the same thing as you? This . . . Sub Rosa secret?"

At the word *abductor*, Colby's grandmother threw her head into her hands. "Please, please. You must do everything in your power to catch this criminal," she implored.

"Mrs. McCracken." Faber passed her a battered box of Kleenex. "I already have an APB out on the missing parties. But within the privacy of this office, I've got every reason to believe that this mystery kidnapper doesn't even exist." And with another hard look at Noodle, she opened a binder and pulled out a photo of the same leather-bound copy of *The Alchemy Treatise* that they'd seen at the Metropolitan Museum.

"Two days ago," she continued as the photo made its way around the room, "this book was stolen from the Keller exhibit at the Met. It's valued at a quarter million dollars."

"Hold up!" Noodle popped up from his chair. "We didn't have anything to do with that—"

"The very same book," interrupted Faber, "that Mrs. Edison found in her son's bedroom this morning."

Noodle turned toward Tom's mom, whose unhappy face confirmed it.

"Mrs. E! We're being framed here!"

"I saw it with my own eyes, Bernard."

"I'm telling you, it was the kidnapper from the pet shop. He probably planted it or something."

At the word *kidnapper*, Colby's grandmother burst into a new round of fresh tears.

"Detective Faber, my son's not a thief," protested Tom's father, shifting uneasily in his chair. "We're not sure how the book—"

"I'm sure he's not," Faber answered calmly. "Which is probably why he ran away. Have there been any big changes at home? Some reason he'd be acting out?"

"His father just took a job in Kansas," said Mrs. Edison. "Tom isn't taking the news very well." Lieutenant Faber nodded, as if that were exactly the kind of information she'd expected.

"You guys aren't listening! We're being framed!" Noodle was shouting now, and had to sit on his hands to keep from hopping out of his seat again. But no one was paying him much attention. All the adults seemed to be on Team Faber.

"Sometimes difficult situations cause people—especially young people—to make rash decisions," the lieutenant continued, undaunted. "I think Tom and Colby have realized the nature of their crime and are hiding."

"Noodle, please tell us where Colby and Tom are," Colby's grandmother pleaded. "I promise, we won't get angry."

"For the last time"—Noodle tried to speak evenly, but it was hard to keep his voice from cracking with emotion—"they were kidnapped."

"Enough already with the theatrics, young man," Noodle's mother scolded. "You're in hot enough water as it is."

Amid all of the others' commotion and emotion, Tom's father remained strangely silent.

"Right now, the important thing is to stay calm." Faber folded her hands together. "We've got a lot of our officers out there, but I'm certain your kids will resurface soon."

The adults nodded. Noodle clenched his fists. He'd find his friends, without their help. He had to.

36
Coming Clean

Just after ten a.m. and here Noodle was, standing hunched on the Edison family's front porch, his finger pressed to their doorbell. He had decided to disguise himself in a trench coat and sunglasses, but now in the light of the new day, the idea felt extremely ridiculous. He probably just looked like a freak.

Thankfully, the only passerby so far had been Anders, the neighborhood's eleven-year-old paperboy, and Noodle didn't care what that twerp thought about anything.

He pressed the doorbell again, then ducked his head deeper into his coat collar as an old couple came speed-walking past the house in their matching purple tracksuits. Noodle thought he saw them shoot him a sidelong, disapproving glance. Or maybe he was just being paranoid.

Finally, the door jumped open. "Noodle!" Tom's dad's eyes widened. "What's with the Inspector Gadget outfit?"

"I'm under house arrest," he responded. "So I had to sneak out. Though I don't think you're in a position to make comments about anyone's wardrobe, Mr. E." As usual, Tom's dad's shirt was untucked, his glasses crooked, his pants stained, and his hair a bird's nest.

With a wave, Mr. Edison beckoned Noodle to follow him into the house, where he was startled to see that the entire living room interior was gone, replaced by brown packing boxes. A hundred memories shot through him: Tom's house at Thanksgiving; Tom's house when he and Noodle had held an Erector Set competition, and half the class had come over; Tom's house during the ice storm a couple of winters ago, when they'd built the best indoor fort, ever, right on this very living room carpet, the only item that had not been packed yet.

"Noodle?" Tom's dad peered at him. "You okay?"

"Yeah." He cleared his throat. Not the moment for nostalgia. "I need to show you something. I'll need a table, though." Which was not happening in this room.

"Kitchen. Let's go."

At the kitchen table, he pulled from out of his backpack the metal box they'd found under the mile-nine marker.

"What is this?" Mr. Edison adjusted his glasses and knelt down to inspect the dented box. Noodle lifted the lid to reveal the strange machine inside. In his opinion, it looked like a souped-up toilet paper dispenser—a mess of wires, wheels, and gadgets propping up a ten-inch-wide spool of brittle, yellowy paper.

"My current theory is it's some kind of telegraph machine," said Noodle, though he didn't really know what to make of it.

"No . . . it's . . . Where'd you find this?"

"So you know what it is?" asked Noodle, sidestepping the question. Down at the police station, everyone had been pretty annoyed about his recount of the midnight field trip into Hoboken, so Noodle'd decided to go with the "less is less" strategy. The less information he gave Tom's dad, the less mad he'd be.

"It's a universal stock ticker," Tom's dad answered after a moment. "Probably one of the first Edison ever designed." He ran a slow, reverent hand across the machine's chrome base. "See the type-wheel shift mechanism there?" Pointing now to a skinny metal pin running along the inside of the machine: "And the screw thread unison. He designed that specifically so the printing operator could keep all the different machines in line." He leaned close to the machine, touching a few of its gears. "This little gem here gave birth to the stock exchange as we know it today." Tom's dad knotted his hands behind his back as he bent forward, preferring to observe rather than tinker.

"Mr. E, I think this machine's the key to getting Tom and Colby back."

"Does this have to do with your kidnapper story?" Mr. E removed his glasses and zoomed his full attention onto Noodle. "I need you to tell me the truth."

Noodle knew Tom would die if he found out his dad was about to get involved in the treasure hunt, but Tom wasn't here now, and Noodle didn't know what else to do.

"All right, Mr. E. I'm about to lay some knowledge on you right now that you might not want to hear. But I need you to take off your grown-up hat for a second and hear me out."

"All ears." Tom's dad took a seat and placed his hands on the kitchen table, waiting for Noodle to begin.

"Remember that photo from the camera?"

Tom's dad nodded warily.

"Well, thanks to some Sherlock-style skills from yours truly, we realized it was actually a clue. To where this really old record and movie film were hidden."

"And where were they hidden?"

"Some crazy lady's pet store in Brooklyn, but that's a whole other nightmare. The point is, the record and movie led us to the train tracks. Where we found this!"

Tom's father leaned back in his chair. His mouth hung open slightly, but his face was impossible to read.

"But that's when the kidnapper dude showed up and took Tom and Colby."

"Okay, Noodle." Mr. E looked up at the ceiling and closed his eyes a moment. "What if I told you that I believe every single thing that you just told me?"

"No way! You do? Then you also think Colby was kidnapped? But then why aren't you—"

Mr. E held a finger to his lips. "We have to stay calm. That's the first rule. If this really is about what I think it's about, then you're right. My great-grandfather and the Sub Rosa have hidden something very, very precious, and other people want it. And if this clue is the answer, or if it puts us closer to the answer, then that's our best leverage for getting Tom and Colby back. We're dealing with some less-than-respectable people, and we need to proceed with caution."

"Then . . . you think you can make this work?"

"What choice do we have?"

"We could go to the police," Noodle offered, but Tom's dad shook his head no.

"If you're telling the truth, that means someone else planted the book. So going to the police with this might only make things worse." The wheels and cranks of Mr. E's mind turned carefully as he worked through their options. "Finding the next clue's our best shot." He went pensive for a long moment, studying the ticker.

"Sometimes it's hard for me to believe you and Tom are related," said Noodle. "He'd have ripped this thing apart by now."

"In this case, that wouldn't be a bad idea. The gears and wires are all misaligned, not to mention rusted. And there's a missing part, right here." He picked up the machine gingerly by its base, as if it were a tea tray. "Come on. Let's take this downstairs."

37
A Slip of History

Two hours later, and the stock ticker had been dismantled, then slowly reassembled. New radio wires were spliced with ancient rubber cables, and each rusty screw and pin had been methodically replaced.

Before reattaching each part or realigning any cog, Tom's dad would study the machine for several minutes, then search his pristinely organized shelf space for a labeled box of dissected appliances, light switches, springs, or whatever he happened to be looking for. At one point, he'd even stripped apart an old blender motor to extract one perfectly sized spring.

"The device is more rudimentary than anything we use today," Tom's dad muttered, wiping his brow with his sleeve. "And it runs on a completely different voltage. But the principle's basically the same, see?"

"Kinda."

Finally, Mr. Edison produced an eight-volt battery that had been buried near the back of a cluttered shelf.

"Let's pray she's still got some juice left," he said, tearing off a length of electrical tape and using it to attach the stock ticker's wires to either side of the battery.

Finally, Tom's dad stepped back from the table to assess the revamped machine. "That should do it."

Noodle checked for some sort of clue or sign, but the stock ticker didn't seem to be doing much of anything. "That does what? What does this beast do?"

"Nothing. But technically it could."

"So how do we know if it works?"

"Well, what I mean is that it's ready to receive information." He pointed to the roll of tape. "But someone needs to be feeding it from somewhere else. Through a telegraph or phone line," he explained. "Which, as you can see, is a null point because it's not hooked up to—"

Tick, tick, tick. So faint. Hardly any sound at all.

Tom's dad stopped speaking.

Tickticktick. Faster now. He and Noodle stared at the machine as if it were from another planet.

A section of paper, only slightly wider than a bubble gum wrapper, spat from the front of it.

"No way." Noodle could hardly breathe.

"Must be some kind of stored electrical pulse," whispered Mr. E. "Amazing."

"Or it's a member of the Sub Rosa trying to communicate with us from the grave."

Once the ticking had stopped, Tom's dad delicately tore off the sheet of paper and held it close to his glasses as if it were a snowflake.

Printed on the paper, in two lines of wavering type, was a message.

"'Through Mercury's gate, you'll reach the backward horse. The circled rose will light your course,'" Tom's dad read. "That mean anything to you?" He turned toward Noodle, his eyes brimming with hope.

Noodle shook his head, which sank both their spirits. "Unfortunately, Mr. E, not—"

Bzzzzzz. The vibrating cell phone on the table gave them both a startle. Tom's dad squinted at the caller ID before answering.

"Hello?"

"Tom, Curt Keller."

Noodle stared as the color drained from Tom's dad's face.

"Mr. Keller, hello." Mr. Edison instinctively smoothed over his shirt. He'd never actually spoken to the CEO of Alset. In fact, before this phone call, he'd been fairly certain that Mr. Keller had no idea who he was.

"First things first," said the silky voice on the other line. "Congratulations on finding the next riddle."

"Next riddle? I'm sorry, sir, I don't know what you're . . . talking about." Mr. Edison put a hand over the phone as he frantically searched the basement for any hidden camera or listening device.

Keller laughed. "Yes, the house has been tapped. Only a temporary invasion of your privacy, I assure you."

"I don't understand. Why would you bug my house?"

"I want you to find me the next clue, of course. And hand it over peacefully," Keller explained. "Tom Junior and the girl are fine. And as long as you uphold your end of the bargain, everything should be smooth sailing from here out." Tom's father clenched his teeth, his face filled with a white-hot rage that Noodle had never seen before—except for maybe the time Tom accidentally incinerated the family's backyard while testing his Weed-B-Gone blowtorch prototype.

"No deal." Mr. Edison's voice was hard. "I just want Tom and Colby home safe."

"I'm one of the richest men in New York," continued Keller, unperturbed. "You'll get your son when I get my clue. Involving the police will only make things worse. We both know that. Call this number as soon as you have what I need. Good-bye, Tom."

38
Urban Labyrinth

Help! Somebody! Quick!"

Tom's fist was throbbing, but he continued pounding on the door. He'd been at it for almost five minutes before he heard a clamoring down the stairs, and then a key was fumbled into the lock.

"Here he comes," Tom mouthed silently to Colby, who crept closer to the door, coiled on her toes, with one long strip of torn mattress covering in her sweaty hands. The other end was looped into a wide circle on the floor.

After a few moments of key jingling, the bolt clicked, and the door creaked open. As soon as Nicky stepped his foot into their trap, Colby pulled the lasso tight around his ankle and gave it a hard yank, knocking him to the floor with a yelp.

"Aaagh!" His face turned beet red while he flopped on the floor like a beached fish. Tom could see his pained expression.

Once Colby had given the nod, Tom pulled a loose bolt from the iron cot frame, setting off a rapid-fire chain reaction—as the cot collapsed to the floor, so did the heavy armoire that the two of them had placed precariously on top of it. The weight of the falling armoire then pulled the mattress-cover lasso even tighter, dragging Nicky a few feet across the floor and squeezing his chubby leg in a taut bear trap.

"You little brats!" yelled Nicky. "Try gettin' out now!" And with his one free leg, he kicked the door shut.

"No!" Tom yelped, leaping over a sprawled Nicky to yank on the doorknob. But it was locked from the outside and wouldn't budge. He could hear the keys jingling in the lock on the other side of the door, just inches away, though they might as well have been on the other side of the house for all the good that did him. Tom yanked again.

Nicky began to laugh behind him.

"Wanna know what happens to kids who think they're

smarter than me?" He had curled his way up to a seated position, and his sausage fingers were slowly working to untie the mattress-lasso knot. "They get dumped into the East River."

Colby meanwhile was crouched at the other side of the room, working one of the cot's iron legs apart.

In ten seconds, Nicky would be free. They had ten seconds to keep this treasure hunt alive.

Thinking fast, Tom ripped off his shirt, laid it flat on the ground, and slid it underneath the door.

Bam! He knocked against the wood with his shoulder until—*clink!* He heard the key fall from the lock, then tugged his T-shirt back with Nicky's keys now resting on top of it.

"Nice try." On his feet now, Nicky lunged for Tom, but Colby—who'd grabbed one of the iron posts—whacked him across the knee.

Howling, the thug dropped to the floor.

Tom tried the first key, but it didn't fit.

"What's wrong?" asked a breathless Colby, now at his side. "Get us out of here."

"I'm trying." The second key didn't fit either. Tom's

hands were wet with perspiration, and Nicky was on his feet again, limping toward them.

"So close!" The fat man was smiling wide. "And yet—" Nicky flailed a meaty paw just as Tom unlocked the door, and in one swift motion pushed Colby into the hallway and locked the bolt behind them.

"I don't think my heart arrhythmia can take any more of this," she said as Tom grabbed her hand, and the two of them tore down the dark basement corridor.

The dull thud of Nicky's heavy body slamming against the door followed them up a flight of stairs that led back into the heart of the townhouse mansion, but this time they were on a different and unfamiliar floor.

"Who'd eat in this room? Yosemite Sam?" Tom paused for a split second as they raced through a lavish dining room. Its polished oak table was at least twenty feet long, and a mounted, shaggy buffalo head stared blankly from above a wooden fireplace.

"Where you two little mice hiding?" bellowed the voice, so loud it shook the entire frame of the house.

"Sounds like Nicky's loose!" said Colby, and within seconds, they were off to the races again, spiraling through an opulent living room; an enormous black-and-white

checker-tiled kitchen; a pantry with cabinets full of porcelain, china, and silver; another short hallway; then finally
into a grand foyer.

Tom gave the front doorknob a desperate rattle. "It's
stuck. Maybe they've got the place on lockdown." He sur-
veyed the corners of the high-ceilinged room. "Though I
don't see any video-monitoring equipment."

"Keller's probably lurking around here somewhere."

"May I help you?" The woman's deep voice made Tom
and Colby spin around to find a uniformed maid standing
at the top of the steps. Her hair was pulled back in a simple gray bun, and her body was shaped like a broomstick.

For what felt like an eternity, Tom and Colby stood
frozen, waiting for the maid to make the first move. The
three of them didn't utter a single word as they stared
deep into one another's eyes, as if all were held under the
same spell.

And then . . .

"Intruuuudeeers!" The maid's screech was as ear-
splitting as an out-of-work opera singer.

"Run!" Tom and Colby doubled back, pushing past the
maid, who grabbed Colby's sleeve for a second before she
yanked it free.

Up ahead was a double-spiral staircase, which they took three steps at a time.

"You can keep running, but it's all a dead end!" warned a voice from beneath them, and Tom didn't need to glance down to know that Nicky was bounding up the stairs and gaining ground.

The mansion's third floor consisted of nothing more than a long, narrow, carpeted hallway with two endless rows of doors on either side.

"Next door, next door!" Colby shouted as they darted through the shadowy corridor and into one of the side rooms.

"Looks like a library," gasped Tom as they entered the stuffy, Victorian study and bolted the door shut behind them. He stalked the room's perimeter, leaning against its high bookcases and tilting old Tiffany glass lamps. Outside, Nicky's lumbering footsteps approached like an earthquake.

"What are you doing?" Colby whisper-yelled.

"You know—the old revolving-bookcase trick."

"This isn't a *Scooby-Doo* episode, Tom. Our best bet is just to be quiet and wait Nicky out."

"Or try one of the windows." But Tom quickly realized the second option was a bust since the windows were double-glazed, iron-barred, and opened onto nothing but the back view of a brick building.

Colby leaned an ear close to the door and was met with the sound of the doorknob jiggling on the other side.

"He's right outside," she mouthed, slowly backing away.

Bam! The two of them winced at the sound of Nicky's shoulder lowering against the door. It was followed by a long and terrifying silence.

"That's not gonna hold him very long," said Colby, barely audible.

Bam! The oil paintings trembled again from the force of Nicky's weight. "Come out, come out, wherever you are!" he sang from the hallway.

"We're dead." Colby stepped behind Tom's body as they retreated toward the corner of the room.

Bam! The door hinges splintered the frame.

"Wait! Maybe not." Tom was squinting at something along the far wall.

"Talk to me. What is it?" asked Colby, but instead of answering her, he ran across the room and felt along a needle-thin crack, which, on first glance, looked like it was part of the dark, velvety wallpaper. As he pressed lightly against it, however, a latch clicked and a section of the wall swung open. Behind the hidden door was a small closet filled with cracked leather books and suitcases.

"This whole house is like one giant time warp," said Tom.

Bam! The door's hinges were almost loose now.

"Tom!" Colby was pointing toward the closet's ceiling, where a suspended length of twine was fastened to a ceiling hatch. "Think it's safe?"

"Maybe. Maybe not. We don't have much of a choice, do we?" He pulled hard on the twine, and as the hatch opened, a collapsible ladder unfolded. Scrambling as quick as they could, the two of them scaled the ladder all the way up to an unlit, cobwebby attic.

Tom pulled up the hatch behind them, just as the study door fell to the floor with a thud.

Nicky had broken through.

39
A Trunk Full of Trouble

This place just gets weirder and weirder," murmured Colby as she stared at the eclectic scenery spread out in front of her.

"Seems Curt Keller's a bit of a pack rat."

The room was enormous but crammed with steamer trunks, armoires, sheeted mirrors that resembled fat ghosts, and old stacked tables and bed frames.

"It kinda reminds me of the *Titanic*." Colby tiptoed farther into the space, spinning a 360 of pure wonder. "So many places to hide."

Tom pried open a trunk. "If we get into one of these, we're sitting ducks."

Then came a loud creaking of the attic hatch as it was pulled down.

Like scared bats in sunlight, Tom and Colby scurried to the far end of the room and skidded onto the floor behind an enormous wooden table that had been turned on its side.

With their faces pressed against the ground, they peered around the side of the tabletop and saw Nicky's scuffed dress shoes stepping gingerly across the floorboards, stopping every so often as he peeked under a cloth-draped couch or inside a footlocker. At one point, they even saw him check a dresser drawer.

"We gotta hide somewhere," Tom whispered after they'd been watching him for a moment. "He knows we're up here. He'll eventually make his way over."

Colby nodded, then army-crawled quietly back toward an open armoire behind them. It was packed with formal clothes that looked as though they were from somewhere around the turn of the last century. There were old tuxedos and puffy, whalebone-hooped skirts crammed together on a wooden clothes rack.

"Inside the dresses," she said. "He'd never look there."

"Colb," Tom hissed back. "There's no way I'm hiding in a lady's dress."

"Yes, you are! One of us can signal when it's safe to

come out." Nicky was getting closer now. "Now get in that dress!"

Yanking the fabric over their bodies, soon both were enveloped by the long, frilly skirts.

Inside his pink cocoon, Tom pulled his knees to his chest and listened. The footsteps were closer, and he could hear Nicky shoving furniture out of the way. A trunk opened. A muttered curse under his breath. Fatty couldn't be more than five feet from the old armoire now, Tom guessed. His every muscle was held motionless. Above his head, a hand crawled through the clothes, giving them a cursory search.

Then the steps grew fainter as they made their way toward another corner of the attic. Nicky was now on the opposite side and, with any luck, Tom and Colby might even be closer to the attic hatch.

Tom knew this guy wasn't leaving until he'd found them, so if there was ever a moment to make their escape, that time had to be now.

"You ready to bolt?" Tom whispered in what he assumed was Colby's direction.

"No, but let's go anyway," she whispered back. "Now?"

"Now!"

They jumped out of the wardrobe. Nicky spun in their direction, tripping over a coatrack as he chased them toward the attic hatch. Colby was the first to descend. Tom's feet accidentally stepped on her fingers as they climbed back down to the study.

"My bad," he said as they bolted into the hallway.

"Every door in this house is locked!" Nicky called after them. "You're only making the punishment worse for yourselves."

"We're definitely making it worse for you!" said Tom.

Out into the hallway again, they flew back down the spiral staircase, then crossed the mansion toward the rear kitchen.

"Wait!" Tom skidded to a stop next to a metal trash chute that opened like an oven door. "What do you think?"

Colby raised an eyebrow. "You wanna go down that thing?"

"Think of it as a very, very smelly waterslide."

"Hmmm. Not comforting." Colby shuddered at the thought, then shrugged. "But I'm game."

"And you realize it probably leads to a humungous pile

of trash, right? With eighty thousand species of germs."
Tom couldn't help laughing.

"Just get your butt in that chute before I change my mind."

"Who are you?" Tom stared at her for a moment. "And what have you done with Colby?"

"Har-dee-har."

Tom flipped down the metal door, and in they dove, headfirst, just like a waterslide.

Swoosh! Their bodies whipped and bent, one flight down to the belly of the mansion's basement, where they dropped into an industrial-size rubber garbage bin.

"Whew." Tom sat up, glancing around the dark cellar. "I was half scared it would lead to an incinerator."

"Can we just get out of here?" Colby looked terrified and squeamish as she brushed old lemon peels and coffee grounds off her shirt. "I smell like a sewer rat."

The small, ground-floor window was their best and only chance of escape. Tom leaped up onto an old water heater and unlocked the latch.

He pulled himself up onto a bustling Manhattan sidewalk, and strangely enough, not a single pedestrian batted an eyelash at the two children who'd just crawled out of the low window by their feet.

"For a moment there, I never thought I'd get to smell that sweet New York air again." Colby inhaled from the bottom of her lungs and stretched her arms wide. "Where do you think we are?"

"I'm guessing midtown." Tom gave a nod in her direction. "There's the Empire State Building right behind you.

"Let's move." He pulled her arm. "For all we know, he's contacting outside security. And I'm never going back to Camp Keller again if I can help it."

40
Reconnected

Tom and Colby lost no time making themselves scarce. They'd run all the way across 34th Street, then eight blocks up Park Avenue, never looking back once, until they'd reached Grand Central Terminal. Its large arches and Roman god facade were a welcome sight. Inside the Main Concourse, they blended into the lunch crowd, who were all scurrying to catch their subway connections.

"I keep thinking I see Nicky behind every corner," said Colby, her head on a constant swivel, as they made their way to a long bank of pay phones.

"I've felt that way ever since Mitzi's." Tom grabbed the greasy receiver and dialed Noodle's cell phone number collect. After a few rings, he heard his friend's voice through the staticky connection, and a comforting relief washed over him.

"Who's this?"

"Noodle! It's me!" Tom yelled as the operator asked if Noodle would accept a call from Tom Edison.

"And me!" shouted Colby.

"Yes, I accept. Where are you guys? Is this a ransom call?" Noodle's voice was shrill with fear.

Tom chuckled. "We're fine."

"What's so funny?" said Noodle. "Do you know how worried I was about you guys?"

"Nothing's funny. You just sound like your mom when you get anxious. It's cute."

"For now, I'll pretend you didn't say that. Then I will administer the beat-down when you get home."

"Did you find out what was in the metal box?"

"An Edison stock ticker," said Noodle, like it was no big deal. "One of the first ever made. Your dad and I've been in the basement all morning, trying to crack its riddle."

"My . . . *dad*?" Tom's heart fell into his shoes.

"Yep, and we gotta move quick, because someone set you up with the cops to make it look like you stole that old museum book about alchemy."

"Wait, slow down, Noodle. Start from the top—"

The phone was then snatched from Noodle's hands.

"Tom, it's Dad. Are you and Colby okay?"

"Dad! Yeah, we're safe. We escaped from Curt Keller's, but one of his guys might still be after us, I'm not sure."

Mr. Edison nervously paced the length of the basement. This was not the type of phone call most parents could ever prepare themselves for.

"Where are you?" Tom's father whispered, careful not to let his wife hear his conversation. She'd peeked her head down a few times that morning, but he'd told her he was just packing up his tools. She didn't even know Noodle was in the house.

Better not to worry her at this point, Tom's dad had told himself.

"We're at Grand Central. What's the next clue say?"

"Stay right where you are. I want you to go to the information booth and find an adult. Preferably someone in a uniform."

Tom exhaled an annoyed sigh. It was such a parent move to focus on all the unimportant details.

"Dad, there's no time!" Tom had no idea how much his father knew about the hunt, but things on Noodle's end definitely sounded complicated. A setup? A stolen book? Safe to assume it all had something to do with Keller.

"Mr. E!" Noodle waved his arms in front of his face like a madman. "Get off the phone." Tom's dad looked at him quizzically. "That Keller guy's probably listening to this whole conversation."

"Tom, we'll talk when I get there. Stay right where you are. And do not try and be a hero. Are we clear?"

Tom was shocked at his dad's new stern tone. He seemed so in control of the situation. He never acted like that. Usually, he let worry and second-guessing control him, and then smiled politely while people took advantage of his kindness and smarts.

"Okay, Dad. I won't go anywhere." It was all Tom could think to say, even though every ounce of him wanted to keep moving and chase down the next clue before Keller.

"Good. I'll be there as soon as I can."

Tom nodded and hung up the receiver.

"What's happening to us?" He turned to Colby as they walked toward the information booth. Both of them were still a bit jumpy. "You're the daredevil now, and I'm the rule follower."

"I think that's probably a good thing. For both of us."

41
Roadblocked

For the second time in as many days, Noodle found himself running toward the Yonkers Metro-North station. Only this time, Tom's dad was the one panting by his side. Noodle had to hand it to him, though: the old guy could move pretty fast when he wanted to.

The two of them careened toward the station and almost collided with a snowman-shaped transit worker. Her body stretched her blue uniform to maximum capacity, and the buttons on her shirt were the exact brassy match to her cropped hair.

"Sorry," Noodle quickly excused himself as he tried to squeeze past her.

"You're gonna kill someone running around like that," she said, righting her balance with an incredulous look for

Tom's dad, as if he were responsible for the boy's dangerous disregard for pedestrian safety.

"We have to meet someone," explained Mr. Edison with an apologetic half smile. "We're just running a bit late, that's all."

"Well, whoever you're meeting's none of my business, but y'ain't gonna make it. That much I can tell you." She shook her head in a slow back and forth to emphasize her point. "I got a broken-down train south of Marble Hill. Fifty-minute backup. At least."

"So what should we do? Catch the train out of Fleetwood?" asked Tom's dad. He was coated in perspiration, Noodle noticed. He better not sweat off too many more calories. Mr. E's body was already close to scarecrow territory.

The woman's eyebrows drew up. "That, or grab a taxi to Morris Heights."

"But . . . that's halfway to Manhattan," said Noodle. "It'll take forever."

"Don't hafta tell me how far it is; I know how far it is," she said as she waddled past them like an irritated duck.

Noodle searched around the station. The sassy transit worker's story checked out. Nobody was waiting on the platform for the train, and the ticket window was dark and empty.

"Come on," said Tom's dad. "We won't get any closer to Grand Central by hanging around down here."

Noodle followed him onto the street, where he was already hailing a cab. Thankfully, it didn't take long for a beat-up yellow taxi to pull up.

Almost every available inch of the car's interior was colorfully decorated with tacky wooden beads and Jamaican flags. A stick of half-burned incense stuck out from one of the air-conditioning vents. Noodle sniffed. Sandalwood. He slid across the vinyl backseat and peered through the scratched window, gray with grime.

"Fleetwood Station, please." Tom's dad told the driver, a dreadlocked Rastafarian with warm eyes.

"Broken-down train, right?" The cabbie winked in the rearview. "I been shuttling people to Fleetwood all day."

As they screeched out into traffic, Mr. Edison pulled out his wallet to check his cash. There was only a single bill inside. A twenty, which would be just enough to get them to Fleetwood. He hoped.

The cab hadn't even hit two greens when the brake lights on the cars ahead of them began to flash, one by one, and traffic slowed to a turtle crawl. A snaking line of cars waited their turn to merge onto the Cross County Parkway.

Tom's dad fidgeted in his seat, his eyes steady on the ever-increasing fare meter. $3.60... $5.90... $7.20... A few more minutes passed, and the cab finally stopped moving altogether. Its idling engine jiggled the straw-skirted hula dancer that was attached to the dashboard.

"Excuse me." Tom's dad leaned toward the driver and pushed his glasses up on his nose. "Is there some other route? We're in a rush."

"You gon' wan' make yourself comfortable, mon. Parkway traffic's been a headache all day," responded the cabbie with the calm of someone long used to traffic delays and diversions. "We'll be here awhile."

"Murphy's Law." Noodle rubbed his eyes with the heels of his hands. "No luck but bad today." He slumped down in his seat. Tom's dad tapped his fingers on the taxi's divider and tried not to think of his son at Grand Central or of Curt Keller, who was no doubt out there looking for him.

"Cool ring!" said Noodle, pulling Mr. Edison from his worried thoughts. "Where'd you get that?"

"Oh, this?" Tom's dad twisted it off his pinkie finger to show Noodle the golden, circled rose pattern beneath the many-sided emerald. "It's a family ring. Never wore it before, but with everything that's happened, I thought it might bring us luck." And with another nervous glance at the fare, he added, "But it sure won't pay for this cab ride, and we're losing time."

He leaned forward toward the cabbie again. "I'm sorry, but would you mind getting off at the next exit?"

"Sure thing," said the cabbie. "But I don't know how else you plan on getting to Fleetwood."

"Don't worry about us. We'll figure something out."

Once they were off the highway, Tom's dad grabbed his few bills of change from the driver and swung open the door. He now wore a determined expression on his face. Like a superhero.

"I have to get to my son, Noodle," was all the explanation he gave.

"I couldn't agree more, Mr. E. But how're you planning to get us to Grand Central—flying carpet?"

"Just follow me."

42
City Beneath the City

Together, Noodle and Tom's dad raced across Yonkers Avenue, then took another left, which put them on Hayward Street, a narrow road just a few hundred yards from the parkway.

Halfway down the block, Tom's dad stopped. His eyes cut back and forth in search of something. Then he stepped off the sidewalk and knelt to examine the tiny opening in the top of a manhole cover.

Noodle scooted closer to watch. "Are you ever gonna tell me what we're doing?"

"If I explain it to you, Noodle, you'll back out."

"Oh, that makes me feel a whole lot better."

Mr. Edison pulled out his ring of house keys and sifted through them until he found what looked like a small, nondescript key, the kind that might open a jewelry box.

"City workers enter the utility vault by using a lock pick." Tom's dad hooked the key underneath a small opening near the edge of the manhole cover. "We'll have to improvise with a regular key. It's just a matter of pushing back ... the ... catch."

Then he jiggered the key until something underneath the cover clicked, and he was able to wedge it up a few inches with his fingers.

"Here. Come lend me a hand."

Noodle squeezed his fingers in next to Tom's dad's and helped lift the cover a little bit higher. The metal was heavy, almost a hundred pounds, Noodle guessed, and it took all their combined strength to drag it over to the side.

Below the street, a paint-chipped ladder disappeared down into the darkness. Noodle leaned over and could barely make out a maze of pipes, ranging from a couple centimeters to about four feet in thickness.

"I used to work for the city as a low-level engineer before I started at Alset," Tom's dad explained as he descended the ladder, "so I know the whole infrastructure back and front. Up and down." He was gone from sight now, but his voice rose, echoing up from the depths of the cavern. "Noodle, hurry up."

Noodle wasn't thrilled about this odd change in plans, but he didn't have a choice if he wanted to get to Colby and Tom. He closed his eyes, grabbed hold of the ladder, and began to climb down. If there was one thing he was accustomed to doing, it was following an Edison down a blind alley toward almost certain trouble and probable injury.

"Wowzie," he said as he joined Mr. E at the bottom of the ladder, which opened up into a tunnel. "We're, like, in the city's basement." It smelled like a basement, too—wet and mildewed, cast in concrete, with pipes crisscrossing all around him and leading out in all different directions.

Tom's dad was busy checking all the markings and symbols that were painted on the various pipes. "Gamma line, check. But we need to follow the beta line. Both empty into the Hudson River," he muttered to himself.

"What do you mean, 'empty into the Hudson River'?" asked Noodle, coughing through the dry lump of fear that had just formed in his throat.

"Each of these submains feeds into a main pipe. Just keep looking for the beta line."

Noodle wasn't sure how that answered his question, but he did what he was told, brushing some rust off one of the smaller aqueducts. Its symbol was a Greek letter that looked sort of like a cursive E.

After a few more minutes of searching, Noodle broke the silence. "I see B," he called, as soon as he spied a large letter B chalked in white across the side of one of the tunnel's larger pipes.

"Brilliant!" Tom's dad answered. "You found it."

With zero regard for his jacket, Tom's dad bent below the dirty pipe to inspect its pressure gauge, his face and hands now completely covered in fine red powder.

"And when will it be an appropriate time for you to tell me what the heck we're doing down here, Big T?"

"We're going to get Tom and Colby, of course." Mr. Edison reached toward a steering wheel–type device that was connected to a small circular door at the top of the pipe, and began to yank it left. "And we're not waiting in an hour of traffic either."

Hissing sounds filled the tunnel. A thick jet of steam shot out from the top of the aqueduct as Tom's dad creaked open the rusty hatch.

"Ah!" he said as he took a deep inhale. "Brings me back

to my days as a junior engineer. Weekends, we'd all get together for aqueduct races."

Inside the pipe was a rushing stream of water.

"Ready to give it a go?"

"I don't even know what an aqueduct race is, but it sounds exactly like something your kid would make me do." Noodle took a couple steps back, unsure if Mr. E was serious with this plan. "And he usually has some pretty crazy ideas."

"Just lie back and relax." Tom's dad grinned. "It's easy."

"Yeah. Piece of cake."

43

Don't Go to the Light...

U h-uh, Mr. E." As he stared down at the rushing water inside the anaconda-sized pipe, Noodle was starting to have second thoughts. "I love Tom and all, but a man's gotta draw the line."

Without paying much attention to his protests, Tom's dad stuck one foot through the opening at the top of the aqueduct, then lowered in the rest of his body. Another moment, and he'd disappeared inside the pipe completely.

"Come on. The water's not even cold." His voice sounded tinny and hollow.

"This is really happening." Noodle shook his head in disbelief as he took a hesitant step toward the aqueduct.

He couldn't wimp out now. Tom and Colby would never let him live it down.

Eyes closed, he placed a cautious foot through the opening. Water rushed into his shoes. Its biting cold numbed his whole leg in a matter of seconds.

"Hold your breath and plunge right in," Tom's dad instructed from the darkness. Like it was that easy.

"Hawwwwhhhh..." Shin-deep in the foot-high water, Noodle shivered to his core. He swung in his other leg, then plunged himself beneath the opening. Inside the aqueduct, Tom's dad, now shrugging off his Windbreaker jacket, kept himself anchored as the water rushed past his body.

"Double-knot the end of this around your wrist," he said, offering one of the jacket sleeves. Noodle grabbed it, gritting his teeth as icy liquid pooled up around his waist and into his shirt.

"Keep your toes up and your body relaxed," Tom's dad instructed. "Anchors aweigh!"

Noodle sat back in the slow-moving current and let it carry him into the darkness. Soon their bodies were moving through the water at a leisurely pace.

"Huh. Once you get past the initial hypothermia shock,

it actually isn't so bad," Noodle remarked. He was even beginning to relax and imagine how fun aqueduct races with his friends might be, when a faint rumble began in the distance.

"What was that?" he asked, averting his face from the slap of steadily higher-rising wavelets.

"Hold your breath!" Tom's dad shouted. "We're about to merge onto City Tunnel Number One." The water's flow quickly accelerated. At the last second, Noodle gulped in a huge mouthful of air, just as his body whipped down a steep thirty-foot drop, then swooshed around another sharp corner. Water shot up into his nose as he flipped and spun along the pipe's walls, clutching on to the Windbreaker for dear life.

"Half of New York's water . . . travels through . . . this very pipeline," he heard Tom's dad yelling between submersions. "It feeds . . . over nine . . . hundred different—"

Noodle's head was dunked under the water. He frantically tried to resurface but was becoming disoriented, unable to tell up from down.

"*Aaaagghhhh!*" He scooped some air into his lungs, then was swept into a rapid current.

The aqueduct fed into a massive pipeline over ten feet

in diameter. As Noodle's head broke the surface again, he began to cough. He was dazed, waterlogged, not a very good swimmer, and somehow he had managed to let go of Tom's dad's jacket. All around him, rapids roared past like liquid mountains.

"Noodle!" He followed the voice. In front of him, he could just make out the bobbing shape of a head as it disappeared, then reappeared between the foaming swells.

"Mr. E!" He coughed as water filled his mouth.

An undercurrent pulled him beneath the river surface, then hurled him down the pipe. He paddled against the heavy force, losing breath. His hands and feet churning like a blender, he felt like he was going to drown for sure.

"Don't fight the current," yelled Tom's dad. "Just let it pull you."

His body was telling him to panic, but Noodle went against his instincts and stopped fighting. To his surprise, the water spun his body calmly and dragged it with the current.

Out of nowhere, a hand reached through the frigid water to grab and pull him close. Noodle hacked and choked on the air.

"It's almost over," said Tom's dad, just as the pipe took another hairpin twist, then another bend. "My apologies, bud. I assumed you were a stronger swimmer."

"The Zuckerbergs are strictly land dwellers."

Soon, a pinpoint of light appeared in the distance, and the stream rushed them swiftly toward the tunnel's opening.

As they sailed out of the pipeline's mouth, Noodle closed his eyes, held his breath, and prepared for the impact. His body slapped against the water like an awkward cannonball. His arms and belly stung as if he'd just taken a nose-dive into a nettles patch. Noodle doubled over in pain as he sank into the muddy depths of the water.

"Land!" He whooped the moment his head bobbed to the surface.

Several yards to the right of him was a long pier where a huge luxury yacht sat anchored at the far end. Stunned restaurant patrons at a riverside restaurant laughed and pointed at the boy who'd just surfaced.

Beyond the pier, Noodle could make out the sprawling skyline of midtown Manhattan.

"Where exactly are we?" he asked as he awkwardly treaded water.

"Pier Eighty-one," said Tom's dad, seconds before

dunking his head into the river and swimming toward the shore. "Just a quick shuttle ride to Grand Central."

"I hope the MetroCard machine accepts soaking bills," Noodle called as he dog-paddled after him.

They hoisted themselves up onto the wooden-planked dock, and as Noodle staggered to his feet, he could feel his trembling legs almost give out.

"That was . . ." He sighed, unable to rouse enough energy to speak.

Tom's dad stared off into the distance.

"Let's go get my boy."

44
End of the Line

"What if Keller nabbed them?"

"Don't even joke about that, Colb."

"Who's joking?"

Tom and Colby waited by the information booth in the middle of the crowded terminal. Afternoon sunlight was streaking through the old building's massive windows, which gave the marble floor and hundred-foot stone support beams a calm, ethereal feel.

Tom's nerves, however, were stretched as tight as they could go. Every face coming up the subway stairs or through the street doors was unfamiliar and potentially threatening. The longer they waited, the more time Keller and Nicky had to find them. Not to mention the next clue, which Tom had been dying to know since the moment he'd hung up with Noodle.

"Maybe we should head back to Yonkers," said Colby. "At least we know we'd be safe."

"No, my dad said to wait here."

"And your dad is always right," said a very familiar voice behind him.

Tom spun around to find his soaking wet father standing in front of him, along with an equally sodden Noodle.

"Dad!" He jumped up into his father's arms and, for a moment, let himself be twirled in the air like a five-year-old.

"First question," said Colby as she approached Noodle and placed a tentative hand on his sopping curls. "How come you two look like you just fell into the Hudson River?"

"How ironic you should say that," said Noodle with a wide smirk for Tom's dad. "Care to field that question, Big T?"

"Maybe later. For now, I'm just so relieved you all are safe."

"Well, we're not gonna be for long with Keller still

out there." Now that his dad knew about the hunt, Tom figured the best plan was to bring him up to speed. The truth was, he was sure he could use his father's engineering smarts for the next leg of the adventure, whatever that was.

"So what's the next clue say?" Tom asked immediately. As relieved as he'd been to see Noodle and his dad, time was simply a luxury they could not afford.

"Don't even think about it," said Mr. Edison. "This treasure hunt's over. As soon as we get home, I'm calling the police."

"Dad, you honestly think the police will help us? Keller's probably got people on the inside."

"I bet you anything Faber's in his back pocket," added Noodle. "I could tell by the way she was giving me the stink eye in her office." He did an impression of the officer for the others' benefit.

"Then I'll be the one to deal with Curt Keller," Tom's dad answered. "But no amount of treasure is worth putting all your lives at risk."

"This one is!" Tom yelled, so loudly a few commuters turned their heads and shot Mr. Edison irritated stares. "This is our family's greatest secret, and you're just going to sit back and let Tesla's great-grandson walk away with it. Do you even realize what would happen if a guy like Keller got his hands on the formula?"

"We'll finish this conversation at home. With your mother." Tom's dad's voice meant business. "Now march!"

Tom, Noodle, and Colby headed toward the exit doors, but after three steps, Tom couldn't bring himself to move any farther.

"You know what the first thing kids at school say when I tell them my last name's Edison?" Tom asked his father.

"T, don't," Colby whispered under her breath.

"They say, 'Wow. What happened to you?'"

It killed Tom to hurt his father like this, but he couldn't keep the words from coming out. But more than that, he couldn't let the adventure end. Not here. Not now.

"My last name," he continued, his voice choking up, "is just another word for failure."

Mr. Edison didn't open his mouth. He just stood there, silent.

"We're going home, and that's all there is to it," he finally said. "Your safety's the only thing I'm worried about."

Tom closed his eyes. It felt like someone had taken a hot poker to all his internal organs and squished them around.

"Some things are worth the risk," he said, catching his father's unwavering stare as he trudged toward the doors.

"Please tell me we're not going back the same way we came," said Noodle in an effort to lighten the mood.

"I'll put the taxi on my credit card." Tom's dad placed his hands on Colby's and Noodle's shoulders and followed Tom toward the terminal's exit. "Right now we all just need to get home."

As the four of them walked, Mr. Edison couldn't shake the heavy weight tugging at his heart. He'd felt disappointment loads of times in his life, but today was the first time he'd ever seen that same disappointment in his son's eyes.

He made a silent promise to do better. He didn't want his only son growing up with the same feelings of failure that he carried with him every day. That would not be his legacy.

"...and the terminal's celestial sky was painted in nineteen twelve by the artist Paul Helleu." Mr. Edison overheard a tour guide passing by with a group of old ladies, who were all snapping photos like machine guns. Their heads were craned upward to take in the terminal's green-blue ceiling mural that was peppered with stars and gold-shaded drawings of zodiac characters—the Gemini twins, the Taurus bull—all gazing blankly down onto the concourse.

"But due to an embarrassing error on the artist's part, the entire celestial map is painted backward!" continued the tour guide. "The Vanderbilt family, who commissioned the piece, joked that Helleu was painting the night sky from God's point of view."

Tom pushed through the crowd of eager tourists and exited Grand Central Terminal.

It was impossible for him to accept that the hunt was over—that everything he'd worked so hard for, all the dangers he'd endured, it was all for nothing. His dad had the next clue, and Keller had the rest. It was too crushing.

This is the fate of the Edison men, Tom thought as they waited in line for the next available cab to take them back to Yonkers.

A small yellow minivan pulled up to the curb, and as the four of them stepped into it, Tom's dad was also wrestling with his decision not to tell his son about the stock ticker clue. Although he understood Tom's frustrations, he simply didn't know what a man like Curt Keller was capable of.

Better to let the authorities handle things.

The van turned right onto 42nd Street, and Tom's dad watched Grand Central's imposing entrance grow smaller in the side-view mirror. It was really was quite striking to look at. The ornate stone-chiseled facade encircling the old clock, the two reclining Roman gods staring up at—

Now which one was it? Mr. Edison wondered. He could never remember. *Zeus? No, it was the one who wore the hat. The messenger god* . . .

As the van continued along the road, the messenger god's name finally came to Mr. Edison, and as it danced around in his brain, he wondered why it sounded so familiar, so strangely important.

Then the answer dawned on him, and the color drained from his face, while excited goose bumps formed on every inch of his body. It was a feeling he hadn't experienced for longer than he could remember. It was a feeling of hope.

"Mercury!" he yelled out of nowhere, frightening the

cab driver as well as the kids in back. "'Through Mercury's gate, you'll reach the backward horse!'"

"Dad, who are you talking to?"

"Turn the car around," Mr. Edison practically screamed to the driver. "We have some unfinished business to attend to."

No, failure would not be his legacy.

45
Partners in Crime

"There's the little twerp!"

Relief washed visibly over Curt Keller's face when he saw young Tom Edison, along with his friends and his father, enter the terminal concourse.

"Let's hope they've got some answers for us," said Lieutenant Faber, who was standing to his left in a sweatshirt and jeans. "Because I don't know how else I'm going to be able to get you out of these kidnapping charges if they come up."

"You'll get me out of trouble if you want those checks to keep coming," said Keller. "And I assure you, the alchemy formula is well worth the risk."

"So do you want me to arrest the Edison kid or not?" Faber didn't like her strange old benefactor too much, but ten thousand dollars a week was certainly worth putting her neck on the line.

"Hang tight." Keller wore a mischievous grin as he flicked an invisible speck of dust from his impeccable Italian suit. "Let's see if old Edison leads us right to it."

"Lemme call in a couple off-duty cops, just in case." Lieutenant Faber grabbed her cell and speed-dialed a few guys she knew she could trust. Guys who, like her, weren't afraid to bend a few rules.

"I hope you're calling someone more competent than that imbecile private investigator you pawned off on me." Keller spun on the heel of his alligator-leather loafer and retreated a few steps from the balcony ledge to make sure he wasn't spotted.

"Hey, Nicky Polazzi's one of the best private eyes in the business," Faber called after him, bristling at the attack. "You're the genius who tried to make your own rules when you had him throw two seventh graders into an unmarked van."

"It was meant to be an empty threat," said Keller. "Just to shake them up."

"Well, it's against the law."

"We've all broken a few laws, Lieutenant."

He'd be happy when this hunt was over and the alchemy formula was safely in his hands. Between feisty police officers and bratty children, it was all giving him quite a headache, but he knew it would be worth it in the end.

Nikola Tesla's revenge was just within his grasp.

46
Spidey Sense

How do we get close enough to see it?"

Tom stared up at the golden Pegasus, the winged horse, that had been painted in the corner of the Grand Central ceiling.

"'Through Mercury's gate, you'll reach the backward horse,'" his dad repeated for maybe the hundredth time in the last twenty minutes.

"We all got that part, Big T," said Noodle with an exaggerated eye roll.

"'The circled rose will light your course.'" Mr. Edison whispered the second part of the riddle softer to himself. His hands hadn't stopped shaking from nerves and excitement.

"What circled rose?" Tom scanned the entire ceiling for some kind of clue, a sign, anything. "I don't see it anywhere."

"The only way to find out what it means is by taking a much closer look at that horse." Mr. Edison took several steps one way, then another, in hope of seeing the problem from a different angle. It wasn't working.

All around them, commuters were flooding the station's Main Concourse as the evening rush hour ritual began. Uniformed police officers had begun popping up all over the place, too, and Tom couldn't help noticing the sheathed guns and nightsticks holstered at their waists.

"Shame I left my web spinners at home," said Tom, letting out a frustrated sigh.

"Like I've always said, nothing's ever easy with the old Sub Rosa." Colby collapsed onto a nearby bench and dropped her head in her hands. It was the second time she'd closed her eyes in almost forty-eight hours, and she could feel herself quickly dozing off.

"Spider-Man, huh." Tom's dad wiped his glasses with the bottom of his still-damp shirt. "It's an interesting proposition."

"Where're you going with this, Dad?"

"Well, I know it might sound crazy, but . . ." His voice trailed off.

"But what?"

"No, never mind. I really shouldn't even be thinking like this."

"Out with it, Big T."

"Well." He paused for a moment. "Remember the Clorox SuperDuperStick patent you helped me with last summer?"

"Yeah, but we couldn't get it to work."

Mr. Edison nodded. "Because I think we didn't use a strong enough binder. Perhaps if we reworked the ratios a little . . ."

Tom felt a small flicker of anticipation zap his stomach. "We'd need to find Zytrol somewhere, though. And oil, resin. Some sort of compound to make rubber."

"And a hot stove." Lost in thought, Mr. Edison rubbed his forehead and paced away from the group about ten yards.

"Plus, it'd be dangerous," said Tom, catching up to walk alongside him. "I'm not sure I could get high up enough before the solution—"

"Oh, no. You wouldn't be the one going up," said Tom's dad. "I would."

"You sure that's a good idea? You're old."

"I'm not that old, wise guy." He gave Tom a light smack on the back of the head. Tom grinned. It was nice to see his father so intrigued. It had been a long time since Tom had witnessed that. "And no. I think this is all one big terrible idea, but I'm all out of any better ones—"

"And I have no clue what the two of you are talking about when you speak in Edisonian geek ciphers," Noodle interrupted, trailing them.

"Trust me, it's better that you don't," Tom called back as he scanned the concourse for some place where they might find the necessary ingredients for SuperDuperStick. "What about that restaurant?" he said, pointing toward the Oyster Bar at the end of a lower walkway, just off the Main Concourse. "They've gotta have stoves at a fancy place like that, right? And maybe the ingredients we need."

"It's worth a shot," said his dad.

47
Chef Edison

"Fifteen minutes is all we ask, then my son here and I will do your dishes for the rest of the night."

The Oyster Bar's bearded head chef, who looked more pirate than cook, held Mr. Edison's stare for a long moment, trying to figure out whether or not this was some kind of joke. This was one of those times Tom was thankful his dad had such an innocent face.

"All right," the cook finally said. "It's a real strange request, but I know a good deal when I see one."

"I could tell that just from looking at you," Tom's dad said.

"I'll give you these two burners and any basic pantry ingredients you need for ten minutes. But touch my seafood, I kill you."

"Great. Hands off the seafood. Got it." Tom's dad nodded quickly since the chef looked like he was prepared to make good on his threat. "I appreciate this."

"And once we get slammed with the dinner rush, you and your boy will start in on pots and pans."

"Absolutely."

And with a low grunt, the chef stomped back toward his station behind a massive grill, where his minions sautéed shrimp, fried calamari, filleted salmon, and prepared just about every other edible sea creature.

Wasting no time, Mr. Edison grabbed a large pot and saucepan from the shelf behind him, then added in a cup of oil and waited for it to bubble. A few waiters shot him confused looks as they passed through to grab hot plates of food and drop off orders.

Several minutes later, Tom returned from the rear of the kitchen lugging a can of blue paint, a bottle of Clorox bleach, and a small metal tin of industrial wood varnish.

"Your thirteen dollars got me access to the storage closet. Janitor said I could borrow whatever I wanted." Tom placed all the ingredients onto the countertop. "Zytrol in the paint, bleach in the Clorox, and we can reduce the varnish down to a resin."

"Excellent." Tom's dad gave a thumbs-up, all the while stirring the oil until it was splattering over the edges of the pan. "Now measure me out six ounces of bleach."

Tom did, then dumped it into the large pot. In seconds, the smell of burning Clorox filled the room.

"Yo!" The chef yelled over from across the kitchen with his palms in the air. "You didn't mention anything about stinking up the entire joint."

"I'm sorry. It'll only be another five minutes, max."

The chef didn't look pleased or convinced.

"If he thinks that's bad," said Tom's dad under his breath, "wait till I start simmering the paint."

"Yeah, this one could get ugly."

As Tom carefully ladled six tablespoons of gooey blue paint into a measuring cup, he felt an overwhelming warmth come over him. He hadn't worked on an invention with his dad in months, and he'd forgotten how much fun it was.

"The Zytrol's ready when you are," he said.

48
The Whispering Gallery

T his is sooooo super boring."

Colby leaned against one of the many vaulted arch-ways outside the Oyster Bar and let out a huge yawn. "They're taking forever in there."

"When did you become Indiana Jones?" Noodle asked. "The Colby I know used to have germ-induced panic attacks at recess."

"A: that was one time when the pollen count was par-ticularly high. And B: the old Colby had never climbed through hundred-foot-high museum vents or been chased by a maniac through Brooklyn, run down by a speed-ing train, kidnapped, then chased again by said maniac through some freaky haunted mansion."

"Touché," said Noodle with a small eyebrow raise, then went back to amusing himself with another round of people watching. "Check out this guy coming in off the Metro-North. He's totally rocking out on his iPod like he's alone in his bedroom." Colby was about to walk over and help him make fun of the singing freak when—

"You're kinda weird," came a ghostly voice from behind her head. She turned toward Noodle.

"Why'd you just call me weird?"

"I didn't, dork. Even though it happens to be true."

The ghostly voice behind her giggled.

Colby spun onto her hands and knees. Perhaps it was lack of sleep, but if she didn't know any better, she'd have sworn the wall was speaking to her. Slowly she peered close to the base of the archway.

"Who are you?" she whispered.

"Look behind you," said the voice.

She turned. Standing about fifty feet away from her was a little boy, both hands in the air, waving. Colby stared back at the curving wall.

"How am I able to hear you?" she asked.

"Because it's the Whispering Gallery."

"Who are you talking to?" A confused Noodle approached with caution. "You just became way more interesting to watch than any of the weirdo commuters."

"I'm talking to him." She nodded across the archway, then to prove her point, cupped her hands around her mouth and leaned close to the wall. "Say something for my friend."

"He looks like a poodle," said the voice.

Noodle squinted his eyes to make out the little boy.

"I'm twice your size, punk," he whispered.

Another echoing giggle.

Colby stepped out into the middle of the archway. "It's like perfect acoustic symmetry. The pressure waves from our voices must be internally reflected somehow."

"Colb!" Noodle's mouth was wide open. "Didn't that old record say something about a whisper?"

It took her a moment to realize what he was talking about.

"Oh, yeah!" Colby clapped her hands together. "It was like, 'My whisper takes you to the place,' then something about being right below your feet."

"Right, right, but it kept repeating the whisper part."

Noodle followed her, snapping his fingers to an unheard waltz, trying to recall the song. "Then hop on a railway cart, remember? To some secret suite."

"Our secret suite."

"Yes!"

The little boy scurried away toward a woman in a business suit, who was talking on her cell outside the Oyster Bar.

"What do you think it means? Our secret suite?" Colby now approached the other side of the archway and ran her hand along its stone surface, searching for any secret levers, marks, or symbols.

"That there's a hidden room somewhere around here, obvi," said Noodle as he walked to the middle of the archway. A few businessmen brushed past him.

"'My whisper takes you to the place, I'm right below your feet,'" Colby said to herself as she turned her gaze toward the ground. "Right below your feet," she repeated.

The floor was dark with square tiles. Nothing out of the ordinary, except...

"Noodle, what are you standing on?" Colby raced over

and pointed at his sneakers, where a sliver of shiny yellow peeked out from beneath his soles.

He stepped back to reveal a gold-plated, encircled rose that had been laid into the floor. It was smaller than a DVD.

He crouched down to inspect it. "Thousands of people probably walk over this thing every day and never think twice about it."

"So if it's right below our feet, the clue must be in the floor?"

"Except the song says to hop a railway cart," added Noodle. "It doesn't make any sense."

At that moment, almost like a sign from the heavens, the terminal rumbled with the sound of a train departing the station.

"There's our answer."

"Oh, God." Noodle shook his head. "More railroads?"

"It's worth checking out." Colby was already jogging toward the railway stairs without waiting for a response.

Noodle raced to catch up with her. "Not to sound like, well, *you* or anything, but shouldn't we wait for Tom and his dad?"

"I'm very good at spatial geometry, Noodle," she answered. "I don't need Tom to help me find out where the spot is. Plus they've got their hands full."

She continued on toward the stairs, and before Noodle could do anything to stop her, she had already disappeared out of the terminal.

49
Unlikely Hero

From his pocket, Tom's dad whipped out a fresh pair of latex gloves that he'd grabbed from the Oyster Bar kitchen and slid them on.

"I don't feel right about doing this without finding Noodle and Colby first," he said as he took off his loafers and placed them upside down on the bathroom floor. Tom meanwhile swirled the still steaming, gooey blue liquid in a Styrofoam cup.

"Don't worry, Dad. Wherever they went, I'll find them," Tom assured him. "Besides it's you and me Keller's after."

Mr. Edison nodded slowly. His son had a point, and time was not their friend right now. They had ten minutes until the solution dried completely.

The two had locked themselves in a public restroom stall for privacy, but the ammonia-like stench of the SuperDuperStick solution was sure to draw some suspicion.

On his father's signal, Tom poured the contents of the cup first onto his dad's gloves, then onto the soles of his discarded shoes.

"The longer it sits, the stickier the solution gets." And as his dad stepped back into his goo-smeared loafers, they made a loud *glip-glop* sound, sticking to the floor but leaving no mark, thanks to the solution's gelatin-like properties.

"So you gotta move fast." Tom unlatched the stall door and followed his father out of the bathroom.

But as they stepped into the Main Concourse, a new fear gripped Tom. Had he pushed his father too far?

Digging up old artifacts was one thing, but scaling the Grand Central Terminal wall, in front of hundreds of people, including police—that was a whole other level of insanity.

"Chin up," his dad said suddenly, as if he knew exactly what Tom had been thinking. "Remember, your double-great-grandfather performed thousands of failed experiments before he perfected the lightbulb. We can learn a lesson from him."

"And that lesson would be?"

"Never give up."

"Right." Tom wanted to add that testing the lightbulb probably didn't involve any death-defying stunts—not that his warnings would have changed anything. His father was in his own world now, moving purposefully, his shoes quacking against the terminal's tiles as they stepped out into the concourse.

"I want you to go find the others, okay?" his father whispered under his breath.

"And what if something happens to you? Or you need me?"

"At the very least, I'm going to get in some trouble for what I'm about to do." Tom's dad stared into his eyes, letting the weight of this statement sink in. "So whatever happens, you all need to be far away from me. And stay close to any police officers or security guards."

For the second time that day, Tom nodded obediently, which made his father smile.

"You're a brave young man, Tom. I'm real proud of you."

"Just please be careful, Dad." Tom felt like he could

throw up from how nervous he felt. "I'm sorry I brought you into this," he blurted.

"This was my decision, Tom. And I'm happy you fought me as hard as you did."

Mr. Edison held his son close for a long moment, then walked on his goo-smeared shoes in the direction of the huge tan support beam that led up toward Pegasus.

He was a tiny spot in the distance now, all the way on the other side of the massive concourse. Tom shielded his eyes as his father placed a gloved hand on the wall, then another. Followed by a left foot. And a right foot.

He was about ten feet off the ground before the first pedestrian noticed him, but it didn't take long for a small crowd to gather and watch this much less graceful version of Spider-Man scale the wall.

"You crazy, guy? You're gonna get yourself killed!" a college student wearing an enormous backpack yelled as he crossed the concourse toward the subway.

"How's he doing that?" remarked a squirrelly gray-haired woman.

Tom knew he had to go find Noodle and Colby, but he couldn't take his eyes off his dad.

Now thirty feet in the air, Mr. Edison tried not to

look down at the cluster of rowdy gawkers who were clapping and cheering from below. Everyone seemed to have forgotten about their commutes and transfers for the moment.

"Grand Central Main to base. Got a public disturbance in progress!" Tom's dad heard another voice yell above the others and immediately knew it was a policeman calling for backup. No matter what the outcome, there would be no smooth-talking his way out of this one.

This was by far the craziest stunt he'd ever pulled in his life, and though he was certain he'd end up in jail for it, something kept him climbing. Part of it was that disappointed look on his son's face when he'd told him they'd have to give up the search; the other part was a nagging desire to finally achieve something memorable with his life. But none of those swirling emotions could keep him from sweating through his clothes as he came within an arm's reach of the golden Pegasus. It was even more beautiful up close, and its sheer size left Mr. Edison staring in awe.

"Sir! You are in violation of at least a dozen different safety codes!" The bullhorn made a fog of noise in the station's echoing acoustics.

The Pegasus was only a foot from his grasp. He placed

another hand along the curved edge of the ceiling, terrified. His body was almost completely inverted, and he knew the moment he looked down, he would lose the courage to keep going.

With each passing second, it was getting more and more difficult to pull his hands and shoes from the plaster. The solution was drying! If he didn't get down off the ceiling in the next four minutes, he'd be stuck up there for good.

Up close, the horse's gold-painted face was bumpy from the texture of the ceiling, and Mr. Edison noticed a small hole where its eye should have been.

He leaned forward to inspect it. There was something about the shape of the horse's eye cavity that struck him as familiar. Its sharp angles almost made it look like a missing puzzle piece, like something belonged in that empty space.

"'The circled rose will light your course,'" he whispered to himself like a mantra. "The circled rose, of course!" Laughing, he unsheathed his hand from the latex glove so he could scrounge around his pocket for his grandfather's Sub Rosa ring.

He took it out, holding its emerald face and circled rose design to the waning light before stretching to insert it within the pupil of the horse's eye. Miraculously, the ring snapped into place with a soft click.

Mr. Edison backed away, waiting for the magical explosion or fireworks that he knew were coming, but to his surprise, the Pegasus didn't budge.

Ten more seconds. Nothing.

Maybe the mechanism is broken, he wondered. *Or it got destroyed during a renovation.* Since he had no idea what to expect, he had no idea what could have gone wrong.

His entire body trembling, Mr. Edison turned his neck to glance down at the grand marble-floored concourse. There was a crowd of a hundred people gathered now, including at least fifteen police officers and security guards, watching his every move.

He struggled to lift his hand to retreat back down the wall, but like the Pegasus, the SuperDuperStick solution wouldn't budge either.

Mr. Edison was stuck. One hundred twenty feet above Grand Central Terminal.

50
Familiar Terrain

Track 107 was peppered with passengers waiting impatiently to catch the Metro-North local to New Haven.

As they weaved through the crowd, Colby kept glancing up at the ceiling to get her bearings. It was almost as if some internal homing device was guiding her size six sneakers.

"Okay," she said, stepping out onto the train platform and pointing a finger into the shadows. "This track's directly in line with the Whispering Gallery." She paused for a moment, double-checking the calculations she'd made in her head. "I'm guessing the next clue's gotta be somewhere in that tunnel. You up for a repeat performance?"

"And you really think some Sub Rosa mystery cart is

gonna be there waiting for us?" Noodle peered over the edge of the platform. "That seems highly unlikely."

"When have we ever known what to expect from these guys?"

Several yards down the platform, two plainclothes police officers, Sergeants Gilbert and Mancini, kept their eyes trained on Colby and Noodle. They were rumored to be two of the most crooked cops in the department, which was why they were the first two cops Lieutenant Faber thought of to help her keep tabs on these elusive kids.

"What's the freckly one doing now?" Gilbert, a thick-limbed man with a lumberjack's build, turned to his shorter, olive-skinned partner.

"Just hang back," said Mancini. "They got nowhere to go till the train comes."

"Is that a fact, Einstein?" Gilbert smacked Mancini on the back of the head seconds after watching Colby and Noodle jump off the four-foot-high platform and disappear into the darkness of the station tunnel.

Several worried passengers shouted after them, but Mancini and Gilbert were the only two who leaped off the platform and chased them down the railroad tracks.

"Thirty-six, thirty-seven . . ." Colby counted out her

steps while they ran. "Here." She stopped. "This is exactly the spot."

Colby could barely make out faint outlines of the gravel bed and black-walled tunnel as they ran.

"You seeing anything?" she called out into the dark.

"I may have just saved us. Yet again," Noodle answered, seconds before dropping to his knees and running a hand along a tiny crawl space chiseled into the tunnel's bricks. It was no higher than their knees.

"Either that was built by the Sub Rosa or one giant, freaking rat," he said.

"A rat with really strong teeth," Colby said as she began to crawl straight into the narrow passageway. "Only one way to find out, I guess."

"This isn't going to end well," said Noodle, taking a couple hops to psych himself up and ducking his head to follow her through. "Not well at all."

If there was a color darker than pitch-black, this was it. Neither of them could even make out their hands and knees as they dug into the damp pebble- and soot-covered ground.

"This feels like the catacombs," said Colby after they'd

been crawling for a while.

"I know. I bet we're touching skeletons right now"—Noodle let out his most ghoulish cackle—"of all the people who tried to steal Edison's secret before us."

"I'm way more scared of making skin contact with mouse droppings."

"Oh, nasty, Colb."

A few yards farther, the narrow crawl space finally opened up into a larger, high-ceilinged cavern.

"Train tracks!" Noodle shouted into the darkness when his hands brushed up against the metal rails.

"Let's follow them." Colby popped to her feet and, after grabbing Noodle's hand, walked with slow, careful steps along the broken and decayed tracks.

"Ow!" She collapsed suddenly as her knee made contact with something solid.

Noodle reached out a blind hand and felt a metal lever in the darkness, which rolled away with a mournful groan when he pushed against it.

"Colb! I think it's the railway cart."

Their eyes had adjusted a tiny bit now to the dark, and they could just make out a simple wooden plank on steel wheels with what looked like a playground see-saw attached to its top. The metal was rusted over and flaked at the touch, and the wood was bent, moldy, and warped.

"Wish I had one of these bad boys at my house," said Noodle, wobbling to a stand up on the plank. "I'd totally cruise around Yonkers on it."

"Hold it right there!" A gruff voice penetrated the darkness. "Put your hands where we can see 'em."

Colby squinted into the face of the two flashlight beams that were tracking steadily toward them.

"Hop on the seesaw, Noodle!" Colby shouted as she gritted through the throbbing pain in her knee and swung onto the far seat. "Go!"

Noodle pumped his legs, flying up into the air, which propelled the squeaky car forward a foot. Then Colby pushed herself up to build more momentum. Up and down they went, the railway cart gaining speed with each push.

"You kids slow or something?" yelled the voice again. "I told you to stop!"

"We have guns!" yelled another voice.

Faster now, the railway cart bumped and lurched along

the rusty track as Noodle and Colby pushed up and down. Headwind was whipping at their bodies, and their legs were growing tired with strain.

"See?" said Noodle. "I told you this wouldn't end well."

"What do you mean? This rocks!"

Their cart was really flying now, and Colby could tell by the swinging flashlight rays that the two men were falling behind them.

"We need to stop this thing," screamed Noodle when one of the policemen's beams happened to illuminate a wall directly ahead of them, where the tracks dead-ended. "We're gonna crash!"

Colby turned her head to catch a glimpse of the thick cement wall, now only twenty yards away. She stopped pumping the seesaw, but the cart didn't slow down.

"Should we jump?" she yelled.

"That's a death wish! We're moving too fast."

"Noodle! What do we do?"

Five feet from the wall, the cart's wheels clicked against a section of the track and at the last second veered so abruptly that Noodle almost pitched over.

The cart careened around a final bend before lurching

to a stop.

"Gotta love the Sub Rosa," said Colby as she struggled to catch her breath.

Moments later, the flashlights reappeared behind them, their light now bouncing against the golden tint of a metal door frame ten yards in front of the railway cart.

Noodle and Colby scrambled off the cart and headed toward the doorway, which opened into a small, musty elevator.

In the dark, Colby's fingers fumbled the gold-plated panel knobs, madly hitting the floor buttons as the searching beams swept closer and closer. But the doors would not shut.

Mancini and Gilbert approached the elevator, both breathless and angry.

"Hey, you guys aren't packing heat?" asked Noodle, once they were close enough to see.

"Doesn't matter. You two brats are still coming downtown with us," Mancini answered with a smug grin, flashing his silver badge.

"Let's go." Gilbert gripped Noodle forcefully by the arm. "How did you two even know about this place?"

"Lucky guess?" Noodle offered weakly as Gilbert

dragged him away by the elbow.

Mancini motioned for Colby to pass, but as she exited the elevator, she noticed a small golden circle next to the elevator panel, with the word *Excelsior* scripted on a brass plaque above it.

She placed her hand on the gold circle, sliding the latched piece of metal to the side to reveal a small light switch underneath.

"Let's go, princess!" Mancini snapped. "While we're young."

Curious, she flipped the switch on, but nothing happened.

"Strange," she said to herself after Mancini had none-too-gently shoved her out of the elevator. "I wonder what light that was supposed to turn on."

51
A Gift from the Bambino

Out of nowhere, emerald light shot from the winged horse's eye, surprising Tom's dad as it bathed the entire terminal in a soft green that gave it an otherworldly glow. The emerald beam descended in a perfect line, connecting the Pegasus to the top of the four-faced brass clock above the station's circular information booth.

Every single person standing in the concourse gasped in collective wonder, and then the whole giant crowd went silent. All of their faces were turned toward the ceiling, and the only sound came from the whirring motors of the escalators.

"Tom!" His dad called down from the ceiling, his finger pointing toward the terminal clock. "The circled rose will light your course!"

He didn't even need to say anything, though, because Tom was already sprinting toward the information booth as fast as his feet could carry him. Up ahead, he could see Curt Keller's wiry frame vaulting the balcony stairs, and to his left Lieutenant Faber was pushing her way past pedestrians.

Tom leaped onto the information desk, sliding along its glassy surface past two confused attendants until he was face-to-face with the clock. Circling its wide base, he noticed that a thin door, no taller than his baby sister, was slightly ajar. It must've been opened by some unseen mechanism built into the clock.

"Fifteen years I been working here," gasped one of the attendants as Tom crouched down and pushed the mini door open a little wider. "And I've never even noticed that little hobbit door."

"Must be some Keebler elves living in that clock," joked the second attendant.

Nestled inside was an old Louisville Slugger baseball bat, browned and grimy from use. Tom snatched it from the clock's base and crawled to the other side of the booth, ducking out of Keller and Faber's sight. An inscription was burned into the barrel of the bat, just under Babe

Ruth's signature. But there was no time to read it.

As Tom peered over the desk, he was met with a familiar face.

"I should thank you once again for doing my dirty work." Curt Keller reached out a bony hand to grab Tom's arm, and without thinking, Tom wound up and cracked the old man's ribs with the bat.

Slipping out of his grip, Tom hurdled over the desk and tore off down the concourse.

"Thief!" Keller shouted, and in the blink of an eye, an army of security and police were chasing after him. Tom skidded along the floor, eluding two uniformed guards before breaking toward the escalators. Down he ran. There was daylight on the lower floor, until two officers stepped into view at the bottom of the stairs.

Tom hurdled over the side and leaped onto the up escalator, only to see Lieutenant Faber was now at the top, waiting for him.

He was trapped on all sides, every escape route cut off. Tom walked up a few steps, clutching the bat in his sweaty hands. He glanced down at its inscription: *Here your search will terminate. So pop the cork and celebrate!*

Down the escalator continued. If he was going to solve

this riddle, he had to do it right now. Tom's eyes darted for an escape while his mind raced. This was the end of the line.

Here your search will terminate? What did that mean? What was his double-great-grandfather trying to tell him?

He couldn't figure it out.

"Okay, okay. You got me." Tom raised his hands just as the stairs dropped him off right in front of Faber. She calmly held out a hand for the bat.

"I believe that's stolen property."

"Lieutenant Faber, wait!" Tom protested, stepping back as Keller limped to her side. "You don't understand what this guy's after!"

But he understood in one look that Faber's loyalty rested with the bigwig CEO, not the troublemaking seventh grader.

Faber took another step toward him, causing Tom to retreat a few more feet. The baseball bat was now tucked behind his back, out of view. His fingers crept along the top of the barrel, where he could feel a small indent at the top.

Pop the cork!

"I'm through playing games here, Edison." Faber shot him a dark glare as Tom retreated several more steps, buying a couple precious moments as his fingernails pried a cork stopper from the top of the bat. A tiny metal object, about the size of his pinkie finger, fell softly into his palm. Tom quickly replaced the cork and tucked the piece of metal inside the cuff of his shirt seconds before an approaching police officer ripped the bat right out of his hands.

Like a loyal Labrador, the officer handed the bat to Faber, who presented it to Keller.

"Nice work, Lieutenant," said Keller, turning the bat over in his fingers.

"'Here your search will terminate. So pop the cork and celebrate,'" he read, then knocked the bat's barrel with his fist, holding it to his ear as if he were expecting it to whisper the Sub Rosa's secrets to him. "Hard to believe a lifetime of searching ends here, eh?"

Tom did his best to look hopelessly crushed, even though his heart felt like it was about to burst through his chest. He prayed Keller wouldn't discover the cork at the top of the bat. At least not until Tom was safe at home with his dad, although the chances of Keller cracking the next clue anytime soon didn't seem too likely. Keller's greatest asset was also his weakness: he paid other people to do his dirty work.

"Nothing personal, kiddo," said a gleeful Keller, and he was about to turn toward the exit with Faber when something stopped him. "Ah, who am I kidding?" he added with a cocky shrug. "It's a little personal."

At the other side of the terminal, a team of firefighters flooded through the doors carrying several extended ladders to rescue Tom's dad.

"We're not done with you, son." A cop grabbed Tom by the collar and led him toward a waiting squad car out in front of the train station. As they pushed him through the main doors, Tom kept his eyes on his dad for as long as he could.

He was so far away, though, that he couldn't even make out his father's sad smile.

52
The Final Clue

Spring break was drawing to a close.

Tom, Colby, and Noodle waited quietly around the kitchen table for Tom's mom to return from Manhattan's Midtown South Precinct, where Mr. Edison had spent the last day and a half, answering questions about how he ended up hanging from the ceiling of Grand Central Terminal.

Just like the three kids had done, he told them everything he knew: how they were in search of Thomas Edison's secret formula to create gold, how Lieutenant Faber had planted the stolen book in Tom's room, and how Curt Keller and Nicky Polazzi had been the ones who'd kidnapped Tom and Colby.

The detectives didn't believe a word about any secret

alchemy formula, but since so much of their stories checked out, they had no choice but to order a department-wide investigation on Faber, as well as on Sergeants Gilbert and Mancini, and have a judge issue a restraining order on Curt Keller for the time being.

But the old CEO's whereabouts were currently unknown.

The sound of keys jiggled in the lock, and Tom's parents entered the kitchen. His mom set Rose down and headed toward the fridge to make her lunch. She looked tired, Tom noticed. Not that he blamed her. She'd had the scare of her life when Tom went missing and now had to deal with fines, cops, and a delinquent son and husband.

Since it was their second strike with the police, Tom, Noodle, and Colby had been given mandatory community service, and their families each had to pay a five-hundred-dollar fine. Still, they hadn't been sent to "the big house" as Noodle had feared, and had even received an e-mail of appreciation from the mayor for their help in uncovering an elevator that supposedly led to a private room in the Waldorf-Astoria Hotel next door. What exactly that "secret suite" was, the kids had no idea.

Tom's dad took a seat at the table. Nobody spoke.

Noodle finally broke the silence in typical Noodle fashion. "So you beat the rap, Mr. E?"

"Decent fine. License suspended," he answered with a sigh. "All in all, though, I'd say I got off easy."

Tom's relieved eyes met his mom's. She smiled. Or at least it looked like a smile. It was hard to tell with her sometimes.

"Your father explained everything on the way home from the station," she said. "I'll just never understand how the two of you get yourselves into these situations."

"But," Tom's dad piped up, "your mom and I have also decided that even though the outcome wasn't what we'd hoped, the adventure itself had given us something."

He reached across the table and placed his hand over his wife's. "Something this family had been missing for a while, and I think, when we're in Wichita, that we need to remember how—" He broke off, confused. "Tom, what are you smiling about?"

"You've got exactly the look on your face that always worries me," added his mother. "So spit it out. What do you have to tell us?"

All eyes were on Tom, who grabbed a notepad and

started writing, then slid it across the table toward his father.

Here your search will terminate. So pop the cork and celebrate, it read.

"Yeah, yeah, we all know what the baseball bat said," sighed Colby with a glance toward Tom's note.

You're not getting it, he wrote in huge, underlined print, shaking his head no like a mime as he gestured toward the ceiling. Tom was certain there were still a couple of Keller's listening devices hidden somewhere.

"What's to get?" whispered his dad.

Tom then reached into his pocket and placed a tiny metal key on the kitchen table. He'd hardly been able to contain his excitement while he'd waited for his father to come home from the station.

This was inside the baseball bat, wrote Tom.

His dad picked up the key, slowly turning it over in his hands to read its message. They could all now see that engraved into its side were the coordinates 41° 2' 47.42" N, 73° 51' 50.12" W.

"I can't believe you held out on us for this long," said Colby, smacking him on the arm.

"I wanted everyone to be together," he whispered.

Tom's mother scooped up the key and turned it over in her palm.

"Mommy, lemme see!" Rose's round fingers wriggled for it, and Mrs. Edison held it close for her daughter to get a good look.

"Pretty," Rose pronounced.

Tom's dad sprang to his feet. He had his Swiss Army knife out and used it to slice open one of the storage boxes that was marked MISC—DESK DRAWERS.

"What are you looking for?" asked Tom's mom. "I spent all week organizing those boxes."

"Something we accidentally packed," he answered.

After a few moments of searching, Mr. Edison pulled out a large map of the United States.

He was determined to figure out where those coordinates led.

53
Biding Time

Splintered pieces of baseball bat were scattered across the entire hotel desk, and Curt Keller was no closer to figuring out the next piece of the puzzle.

Here your search will terminate. So pop the cork and celebrate!

He'd found the worn cork on the top of the barrel, but once he'd popped it, there was nothing hidden within the hollowed-out space.

Had the little Edison brat managed to sneak it out right from under his nose?

Rage filled Keller's brain. It was bad enough that there was a warrant out for his arrest, but now Faber wasn't answering her phone, and neither was that pitiful private eye.

The Edisons had to have the next clue, Keller decided. There was no other explanation.

Stepping into the hotel bathroom, he gave his reflection a hard stare. He was showing his age. The wrinkles around his tired eyes and in his sallow cheeks were losing the inevitable battle against time.

The alchemy formula would be his final fight, and he would not be at peace until it was in his hands where it belonged.

All in due time, he thought. *For now, there are more pressing matters.*

First, he'd have to reach Faber and figure out how to distance themselves from these kidnapping and robbery charges. So many people would have to be paid off, so much evidence hidden. It was exhausting just to think about.

The cops would certainly be looking for the Babe Ruth bat. Fortunately, Keller and little Tom were the only ones who'd seen the Louisville Slugger up close.

It was his word against a seventh grader's.

And once the police were taken care of, Keller could refocus his attention where it belonged—finishing his great-grandfather's fight.

54
The Sleepy Estate

The Edison station wagon crept along the gravel drive and turned between the two columns that guarded the sprawling estate.

According to their research, the house had once belonged to the writer Washington Irving, who had not only written some of the best-known ghost stories of his time but was also one of the Thomas Edison's favorite authors.

"Ya know, I do remember my father having a signed copy of *The Legend of Sleepy Hollow*," said Tom's dad as he followed the parking signs up the winding driveway. "But I think he had to sell it to fund some of his inventions."

"So I guess Irving must've been in the Sub Rosa, too,"

said Tom, taking in all the vivid flowers and overhanging trees that lined the property.

Tom's dad shook his head. "I don't think so. He died when Edison was only twelve."

"Still looks like as good a place as any to bury a secret," added Colby.

His dad parked the car, and Noodle and Colby sprang out, racing each other to the front door. The house itself was a quirky piece of architecture, multigabled with a red tiled roof adorned with copper weather vanes and multiple chimneys. Blooming wisteria vines snaked their way up the estate's stone walls, which made the whole structure look enchanted.

"Mom would love this place," said Tom as he and his dad approached the house's entrance and Mr. Edison paid for all of their tickets.

"Maybe we'll bring her next time."

Tom's mom had only allowed them to follow the next clue under the condition that she didn't get any surprise calls from the police. Even with the promise of the Sub Rosa treasure, she still wasn't thrilled about Tom and his dad making this trip.

Irving's home had long since become a popular Hudson

River Valley tourist attraction, and there was already a small crowd of people gathered for the two o'clock Saturday tour.

Slipping in with the tour group, the foursome was first led past the grand hall and into Washington's cozy study.

"The estate was acquired in eighteen thirty-five and then dramatically improved by Mr. Irving," said Hannah, their beetly little guide, her hands fluttering with excitement while she spoke. "To this day, we have worked to preserve and maintain his spirit of exuberant romanticism."

Hannah then began to recount an anecdote about the origin of Mr. Irving's favorite pen name, Diedrich Knickerbocker. As soon as the old woman turned to putter down another hallway, Tom's dad gave the signal, and part one of their plan was put into motion. It was simple trial and error. All four of them needed to search every single lock in the house, to assess which ones might fit the tiny key.

Certainly not the most effective scheme.

Colby and Tom were the first to break away from the group, venturing into the estate's formal parlor, a room filled with mismatched Victorian furniture and gilt-framed paintings. Its central feature was a lavish stone fireplace with intricate inlaid brick designs and hand-painted clay tiles.

Colby tapped Tom on the shoulder and pointed to a small sideboard in the corner of the room with a simple silver lock. Tom tried the key, but it was a little too big.

"We might need to rethink our strategy," he said, studying the room. "It could take weeks to find all the locks in this mansion."

"Plus that key could open anything," Colby added. "A box, a chest, a secret room that we don't even know about."

"Maybe the answer's hidden somewhere on the film or in the Firestone photo."

"Which, last I checked, are both in Curt Keller's possession."

"Right." Tom stepped out into the downstairs hallway, checking both directions. For the moment, the house was dead quiet.

"I'm gonna go inspect the foyer," he said, just as Noodle and his dad rounded the corner.

"The tour group went out to see the rose garden," his

father announced. "We've bought ourselves some time."

"I did see one of the curators wandering around some-where, but I'm pretty sure he's half blind." Noodle entered the parlor and peered out the window.

"Tom, why don't you take the upstairs rooms?" his dad offered. "Noodle, you go look in the kitchen, and I'll—"

"*Excelsior!*" Colby's voice interrupted them from the parlor.

"What?" Tom followed her voice and found Colby crouched on her hands and knees, peering into the mouth of the large fireplace.

"*Excelsior,*" she repeated, pointing to a tile on the fire-place's floor, where sure enough, the word *Excelsior* had been scripted in a neat vertical hand. It was almost iden-tical to the brass plaque she'd seen in the secret tunnels below Grand Central.

"I saw this exact word in that elevator, too."

"What does it mean?" Tom turned to his dad.

"It's Latin," he answered, bending over to examine the tile. "Means 'higher,' or 'upward.' Something like that."

Tom knelt next to Colby to take in the soot-covered bricks that lined the back of the fireplace chimney. He lifted his head.

"Higher," he whispered.

His eyes cast upward. In the back of the flue, one small black square of tile was almost invisible against the bricks, unnoticeable but for one thing.

The familiar seal of the Sub Rosa was etched into it.

55

A Door in the Floor

Using his fingernail, Tom pried off the ceramic tile. It came off as neat as a lid.

"Crazy." Colby caught her breath.

None of them could believe what they saw. Hidden beneath the tile was a tiny golden keyhole.

"I got a weird feeling that's our match," whispered Noodle.

Colby rolled her eyes. "Gee, how'd you solve that one, Copernicus?"

Tom's father inhaled deeply with nervous anticipation as his son pulled the old key from his pocket.

With a little bit of elbow grease, Tom wriggled the key into the rusty lock and turned it to the right. From deep within the room's walls came several low clicks and grumbles, followed by an eerie silence.

"Okay, that was weird," said Noodle. "The house just burped."

Mr. Edison looked up at the ceiling, then the windows. Something had begun vibrating beneath their feet. He just couldn't tell what it was.

"Tom, watch out!" Colby dove and pushed him out of the way as a small section of floor in front of the fireplace began to lower, foot by foot, exposing a narrow spiral staircase that led deep into the ground below them.

"Man, the Sub Rosa's some sneaky cats," noted Noodle.

Tom's dad pulled a flashlight from his bag. "All right, let's take a vote," he said. "Should we wait and tell a curator about this, or head down those stairs?"

"*Stairs!*" Tom, Colby, and Noodle answered in unison.

"I couldn't agree more."

Mr. Edison quickly ushered the other three past him.

"Keep your eyes peeled and be careful," he said as they began to descend the stone steps. "This house is old."

Around and around they went, deeper into the floor.

Halfway down the staircase, Tom noticed that the dark walls were beginning to grow lighter, until they were almost a bright gold color, while the streaky sunlight from the parlor above them faded with each step.

Finally, the four of them reached the bottom. The air was heavy with a musty humidity and smelled like a root cellar, though it was hard to tell where they were.

From her backpack, Colby pulled out another, smaller flashlight, which cut a narrow beam through the darkness. It caught bits of objects—the reflection of a brass chest, the flash off a shard of glass. It was clear now that they were standing in front of a wide, cavernous room.

"Everyone all right?" asked Tom's dad when he'd reached the end of the stairs behind them.

"Yeah. We're in, like, a storage space or something." Tom found a wall-mounted light switch and flipped it on.

Light flooded in.

"Holyyyyyy..." For maybe the first time in his young life, Noodle was lost for words.

The room was part inventor's lab, part treasure cave, and had not been touched for years. Gold coins, jewels, and trinkets, thick with dust, made table-high stacks.

Shelves of journals, manuals, and books lined the walls, and arranged on top of a long trestle table were dusty beakers and flagons that probably hadn't been used in more than a century.

"We're all gonna be so loaded!" Colby raced toward an overflowing chest of golden rings and necklaces and tried several of them on, modeling the jewelry in front of a dusty full-length mirror.

"Like a pharaoh's tomb." Still unable to form complete sentences, Noodle walked like a zombie toward a pile of gold coins and sank to his knees. "Can't believe stuff like this actually happens to people like us."

Tom turned to his father, who just held a hand over his mouth. Tears were forming at the edges of his eyelids.

"Make sure you remember to breathe, Dad," said Tom.

His father nodded silently before speaking. "How did I almost walk away from all this?"

"I don't know," Tom said with a casual shrug. "But in the end, you didn't."

Colby's laughter filled the room as she dragged Noodle through all of the golden treasures, stopping every few seconds to pour a stack of gold coins through her fingers or to inspect a golden chalice. She was now weighed down with so much priceless jewelry that she could barely move.

Tom walked along the edge of this magnificent room. His father was still standing at the entrance, just watching them.

There was so much to see, and Tom was on a humming, buzzing sensory overload, so he couldn't have explained, exactly, why he was curious about one object in particular. Perhaps it was because the dusty and drab wooden trunk had been pushed so far into the corner and was easily the most unexceptional thing in the room. Tom only noticed it because it seemed so out of place, sitting there alongside so much sparkling treasure.

As he approached the trunk, his heart lurched to see the three initials, same as his own, stamped plain beneath the complicated-looking latch.

He ran his fingers along the lip of the lid and nudged a tiny lever located just beneath the trunk's lock. The padlock flipped down, and Tom opened the box with a creak.

56
The Golden Formula

I think this is..."

Tom's voice died in the air as he stared into the trunk. His father had materialized at his side and placed an encouraging hand on his shoulder.

"Go on," he said. "I think you might be right."

The book inside was beautiful, leather-bound and heavy, with a velvet padding along the inside cover. Its parchment pages were thick and yellowed with age.

Tom turned to the first page, a scripted introduction written with a quill pen.

"'Herein lies what we believe to be the most incredible scientific discovery ever made by man,'" Tom read aloud.

By now, Noodle and Colby had taken a break from their treasure games to squeeze in behind him.

"'By reading on, you accept the responsibility to guard this book's most precious secrets with integrity and the utmost humility,'" he continued. "'And though there will undoubtedly arise the urge to use the formula for one's own greed and wealth, you must never succumb to its intoxicating powers, for knowledge is the most priceless treasure of all.'"

And then, in faded blue ink, was the signature:

Thomas Alva Edison
Sub Rosa Member
23 August, 1912

With shaking hands, Tom turned the page to reveal a complicated-looking formula, one of many, written below several lines of text.

Within the earth's most stable elements, there exists the potential for purification, both physical and spiritual, it began.

"It reads like a symphony on paper," his father said softly as he digested the book's complex equations and diagrams.

For several minutes, none of them spoke as Tom flipped through the book. Every so often, his father would gasp at some particular piece of scientific brilliance or shake his head in awe.

The reverent moment was finally broken by a loud tramping of footsteps that shook the ceiling.

"Someone's back," said Mr. Edison with a nervous glance toward the room's entrance. "We need to get the book out of here."

"Wait! We gotta grab some loot first!" Broken from her trance, Colby unzipped her backpack and was about to start filling it with gold.

"Colby, no!" Mr. Edison snapped. "No one can know about this place."

"Just a couple pieces, Mr. E!" begged Noodle. "Cash flow's a little tight in the Zuckerberg household these days."

But there was simply no arguing with Mr. Edison.

"The book comes with us and nothing else," he said, shaking his head as he watched the kids with intense hawk eyes. "We're the new Sub Rosa now, and it's up to us to protect the secret."

As hard as it was to admit, Tom couldn't have agreed with his father any more.

"Come on." Tucking the book under his arm, he ran

toward the room's entrance. "We really can't afford to get caught right now."

Together they ascended the stairs all the way back to the parlor, where they were met by Hannah's voice, wafting in from down the hall.

"Now, up ahead, we have Mr. Irving's parlor. Which, if you'll look toward your left, still contains all of the house's original furniture."

"Tom, the key!" hissed his panicked father, snapping his fingers. He knew that once Hannah saw those fireplace stairs, her next phone call would be to the police.

Tom fumbled the key out of his pocket, dropping it from his sweaty hands. It clinked against the cement floor, bouncing toward the exposed steps.

With the grace of six years of gymnastics, Colby dove and caught it, her arm extended over the floor's edge, inches above the staircase.

"Nice grab!" said Tom, then snatched the key from her and quickly jammed it into the fireplace lock. He turned it to the left, and the dull rumbling in the walls began again.

From way down below, they could hear the section of floor begin to rise. Not quickly enough, however, as the tour group was now just a few feet from turning the corner and catching them.

"Mr. E, what do we do?" asked Colby.

"Let's get out of here," said Tom, nodding to a door across the room.

Thinking fast, Noodle ducked his entire head into his sweatshirt and raced out into the hallway, waving his hands in the air like an escaped mental patient.

"Beware the ghost of the Headless Horseman!" he groaned at the top of his lungs, frightening the entire tour group. Several old ladies screeched in terror.

"That is not funny, young man," said an irate Hannah. "Not funny at all."

"Where is Ichabod Crane?" Noodle groaned in response.

In the parlor, the spiral staircase had now disappeared—and, along with it, the secrets of the Sub Rosa.

Trying not to laugh, Tom, Colby, and Tom's dad casually walked unseen through the side door and headed back to the car to wait for Noodle, who was busy being chastised by the extremely upset tour guide.

Still, it could have been worse. A lot worse.

57
A New Invention

Journalists and cameramen chatted on cells, texted, Twittered, sipped coffee, and gossiped while they waited for the press conference to begin. Tom, his mother, and Rose, plus Colby and Noodle, stood near the back of the old warehouse and watched as Tom's dad, in his best and only suit and tie, stood at the front of the room fidgeting nervously. It was clear that he wasn't used to so much special attention.

It had been six months since they'd found the Sub Rosa's secret alchemy formula, and in the time since, a reinvigorated Mr. Edison had been quite busy, having secured a bank loan that not only helped keep the family afloat but also provided the seed money he'd needed to launch his new company.

Since then, Tom and his father had spent every waking moment working to perfect their bleach-battery hybrid motor—the one that his dad had always said would revolutionize the automotive industry. From the looks of today's massive press conference, it seemed his prediction was correct.

Mr. Edison was about to announce to the world the official opening of the Edison Motor Company, which would be the exclusive manufacturer of engines using his new fuel-efficient technology.

It would be a risky venture. A lot riskier than using the alchemy formula to manufacture their own private stash of gold, but Tom's father was adamant that their job was to protect the secret, not exploit it.

"We will never use this for our own gain," he'd told them after they returned from Irving's estate that day.

For now, the book was safely hidden in the floor beneath the fireplace in Colby's basement, safe from Keller's listening devices or the long reach of Faber. Neither Keller nor Faber had been heard from over the past few months, but as Tom's father had warned, "We can never be too careful."

Soon, a new treasure map would have to be devised,

one sophisticated enough to uphold the ideals of the Sub Rosa and ensure that its secrets would be passed on to someone worthy of protecting them.

"We'll need to come up with even better clues," Noodle had mentioned the other night. "And our secret society needs an even gnarlier insignia. Something that will reflect our suave, brainy, and daredevil skills for future generations."

But that adventure would have to wait. First, the new auto plant needed to get up and running.

"Thank you, ladies and gentlemen, for making it out to our unveiling," said Tom's father, wiping a drop of sweat off his forehead. "I am so pleased to present to all of you the new Edison Alchemy."

And with that, he whisked a white sheet off the shiny metal engine.

"The first of its kind. A bleach-battery hybrid motor," his dad continued. "Which runs a full ninety percent on electricity and gets one hundred eight miles to the gallon, by our most recent calculations."

The crowd of journalists clapped and whistled, while camera flashes blinked and danced off the engine's chrome body.

A flurry of hands quickly shot up, and Tom's father called on the reporters in order, answering their questions with clarity and a smile for each.

They were interested. They were enthusiastic. They were impressed.

Tom, watching from the back of the room, cheered with delight. He had never felt more proud to be his father's son.

He turned to stare out on the impressive crowd when a tuft of silver hair caught his attention.

From across the room, Curt Keller's stony eyes locked on Tom's, and the old man's blank expression morphed into a devilish, knowing grin.

A shiver came over Tom's entire body as he averted his eyes to the floor, too scared to look back.

Finally, he built up the nerve, but when he raised his head, Keller was gone. It was as if he'd evaporated.

Tom needed to talk to Noodle and Colby in private.

They would have to get to work on finding a new hiding spot at once . . .

Writing Edison's Gold — Fact versus Fiction

The inventions of Thomas Edison were the inspiration for this book. I can spend hours in flea markets and antique stores, inspecting the cogs and switches of dusty phonographs, cameras, and stock tickers. So creating a big treasure map and using these gadgets as clues and key elements of the story seemed like the perfect adventure. One small snag. I knew less than nothing about Thomas Edison, the actual person.

I don't like to conduct my book research on the Internet, so the first thing I did was hit the Santa Monica Library here in Los Angeles. I checked out everything from medieval alchemy journals to Edison biographies to out-of-print architecture magazines. And the more time I spent in Edison's world, the more ideas he gave me.

His friendship with auto tycoon Henry Ford sparked the plot line of a secret society of industrialists, and a heated professional rivalry with the brilliant Nikola Tesla created a natural antagonist.

In other words, the more I researched, the more the story took shape, and the more excited I got about the story, and the more fuel I had to continue my research.

Digging deeper, I found photo archives of secret tunnels and elevators buried beneath Grand Central Terminal in New York City, maps of abandoned aqueducts, and heaps of conspiracy theories. As much as I wanted to send Tom and his pals on a wild ride, what really ignited my imagination was trying to fit together all the moving parts of this giant puzzle. With the discovery of these underground labyrinths, I had my setting—Manhattan. Now it was important to make sure that the train schedules worked, that the geography was accurate, and that the historical folks could really have known each other. Because even though this story is fiction, it's fun to think . . . but what *if*?

Acknowledgments

1. My editor, Greg Ferguson, for guiding me through my first novel and providing such invaluable attention to detail. I trust him completely and am so grateful for his hard work, expertise, and intelligence.

2. My sister Adele, who has taught me more about storytelling than any person on this planet. Whether it's time, money, or love, she is simply the most generous person I know.

3. My sagelike agents, Charlotte Sheedy and Meredith Kaffel, who remind me that the words *tough* and *love* are not mutually exclusive. I am truly blessed to have such warm, smart people in my corner.

4. My amazing and devoted family, Mom, Jody, Rob, Christine, Erich, Squash, Jamie, and Cat. I don't know where I'd be without them. Probably in a mental institute.

5. Lawson, Tim, Gannon, Tyler, Evan, Ashika, Joey, Evelyn, and Sameera. From heartbreaks to health care, you all help me make sense of the world.